WAITING FOR S[

'a fascinating study of male and what breeds it'
— Catherine Stott, *Cosmopolitan*

'dotted with sharp observations and sudden pleasures'
— Ferdinand Mount,
Times Literary Supplement

'notably well-constructed'
— Norman Shrapnel, *Guardian*

'John Braine shows all his usual grasp of veracious detail'
— Phyllis Bentley, *Yorkshire Post*

'a rare craftsman'
— Janice Elliott, *Sunday Telegraph*

John Braine

Waiting for Sheila

MAGNUM BOOKS

Methuen Paperbacks Ltd

A Magnum Book

WAITING FOR SHEILA
ISBN 0 417 02100 3

First published 1976
by Eyre Methuen Ltd
Magnum edition published 1977

Copyright © 1976 by John Braine
(Bingley) Ltd

Magnum Books are published
by Methuen Paperbacks Ltd
11 New Fetter Lane, London EC4P 4EE

Made and printed in Great Britain
by Richard Clay (The Chaucer Press) Ltd
Bungay, Suffolk

Don't you know that the game is crooked?

Of course I know, but what can I do?
It's the only game in town.

It has all been worth while. I regret nothing. I have had my moments of rebellion, I have seen myself as other men see me, and I haven't liked it. I've read a lot of articles about the lack of community spirit in the South-East, the region where nobody knows each other and you don't know that your next-door neighbour is dead until his body begins to stink. I can only say, with a considerable amount of bitterness, that the authors of these articles evidently haven't visited Sugar Hill.

That isn't its real name. It's a suburb of a Surrey commuter town, with about three thousand population, about three miles from the centre. There's a railway station on the main line to London, an Anglican church, a Catholic church, a village hall (for once it was a village), a shopping centre, and a garage. And two prep schools and an almost brand new junior school. Most of the houses are detached, with double garages. There are a lot of trees; in the summer I like to sit in the drawing-room with a glass of lager and the window wide open, the cool night air bringing in the smell of night-scented stock and growing, heavy as the earth, blending with the lighter, faintly wine-like smell of the flowers and the grass.

I hold back nothing, not even what I feel for Sugar Hill (which isn't really a hill but a shallow plateau). Nor Box Common, a sandy heath of about two square miles, where there is a fair amount of box, but far more pine and fir. There's a great deal of activity on Box Common; when you walk past it on the main road at night, not all the little noises you hear are of animal origin. Parents don't let their children go there alone at any time; and any women who walk there alone take a large dog. In Sugar Hill all the dogs seem to be large. To the best of my knowledge, nothing worse than an occasional flashing has happened on the Common; but it bides its time.

I want to tell you about myself, not Sugar Hill, but what I feel about it is part of my story. I feel strongly about it, as I feel strongly about everything. Sheila tells me to take things easy, to cool it. She likes Sugar Hill too, is perfectly at home in it; but she's not emotional about it. At least, not on the surface. At thirty-eight my face is already deeply lined; at thirty-six hers scarcely at all. It's almost frightening in its smoothness and composure. And the smoothness isn't the result of powder and lotions and creams and massages and face-packs; she uses soap and water and sometimes a little powder, and that is all. Her smell is one of the things I'm grateful for; she is very clean, but smells simply like a woman. She doesn't like scent or even scented soap; and in hot weather she doesn't use anti-perspirants, but takes cold showers. When she comes back to bed then I'll swear she smells of running water. I can't describe the smell. No one can. It's a happiness and a coolness and a flowing without hindrance, clear and light, but cool and dark. I like the smell of her sweat – a woman's sweat smells like new bread – and that is another pleasure, lying beside her, when the effect of the shower wears off.

I had not meant to go ahead so far; I had intended to take my story through in proper order. But I also intended to hold nothing back. I'm compelled to reveal everything just as it comes. I cannot keep Sheila out of my thoughts for very long. Let there be no mistake about it: this is a love story. It's a relief to admit that. I have been foolish

8

enough to think of it as the story of an obsession, an addiction, a fixation. But it isn't. It's an old-fashioned love story. Which doesn't necessarily mean that it will have a happy ending. I hope that it does, but I'm not depending on it.

In my job I count every halfpenny. I know the cost not only of everything the shop buys but what it costs to sell. If I buy anything for myself I'm sharp-eyed, mean, and haggling. And I'm bright enough, unlike most of my neighbours in Sugar Hill, to know that there aren't many real bargains, and that bulk buying, for example, doesn't really save money if what you buy is inferior or if it goes bad before you finish it. I'm careful and calculating and cool – but not where love is concerned. If you are to be involved in a love story, a real love story, the only rule is to give, without thought of consequences.

Sometimes I find myself wondering, catching the quick sly smile – lust, contempt and envy – on a neighbour's face as he looks at Sheila, whether the cost may not have been too high. I am familiar with that smile; I'm introduced to someone, they catch my name, the connection is made. Sheila doesn't even need to be there. They all know her on Sugar Hill, and even further afield. Chertsey, Weybridge, Guildford, Woking – the Sheila Seathwaite country; and any day now they'll give it a special colouring on the map.

They all know me, of course. Everybody in the area buys something from Droylsden's stores sooner or later. And I'm on view in the stores, where the goods are sold and the profit is made, every day it's open, including Saturday. Once the General Manager hides himself away behind the scenes administering, then the trouble begins. The staff start thinking they're doing the customers a favour by serving them and imperceptibly cease to be

9

aware of the inseparable connection between their wage packets and the customers. And sometimes bright young men do what the General Manager should be doing – or as much of it as they can – loyally, sorrowfully, protecting their admiration for the General Manager, always, somehow or other, in full view of those who can ask him to retire or, which is more often done these days, kick him upstairs to a consultant post with a nice little office and a private loo and a phone which never rings.

But this isn't the story of my job at Droylsden's, though Droylsden's – as well as Clifford Droylsden, the Managing Director – is an important part of it. The man you see at Droylsden's isn't the real Jim Seathwaite. He's too self-assured, too formally dressed, too energetic, too thorough and meticulous. The real Jim Seathwaite takes over when the General Manager comes home to Eleven, Medway Close in Sugar Hill, has a shower, changes into casual clothes, and sits down with a lager in the armchair furthest from the fireplace. The real Jim Seathwaite is muddled, dreamy, sometimes sits listening to records – nothing classical, pops or musicals – and as he sits there he wonders how long his luck will hold, how long it will be before he's found out.

If Sheila is in, which isn't all that often, then this Jim Seathwaite is absolutely content. I look at her from time to time as she knits or sews or reads, and always after about half an hour there's the first stirring of desire, half pleasure and half discomfort, then I visualise her under her clothes, the small breasts, the wide thighs, the astoundingly large tuft of black pubic hair, and then I switch off, it's all discomfort. I'm wanting the meal before, so to speak, it's cooked.

And I tell myself it's absurd, that I should grow up, that even now I should try to put things straight, to have it out with her once and for all. It isn't lust I feel. I know what lust is like. There are the days, particularly in spring and summer, that I lust after every woman I see who is even remotely bedworthy. Not the teenagers who, even when they're not wearing tatty sweaters and cheesecloth shirts and blue jeans, are to me too gawky, too coltish, no more sexual objects than children are. I prefer mature women, at least Sheila's age, and I prefer women who've borne children. The real smashers, the Beautiful People, the models and the actresses, the singers and dancers, the professional dazzlers, I can't believe in as women at all.

I only occasionally look at pornography now – I said I would hold nothing back – and now can find only one magazine which affects me. It's one which runs a series of pictures of Readers' Wives (and girl friends and sisters and mothers and daughters, I shouldn't be surprised). The photographs are amateur: the most popular pose is naked with the legs apart. Sometimes they're fully clothed but lift the skirts to reveal, in a word, all. Some are plump, some positively fat, some painfully thin, some passable, some positively homely. What they have in common is that they're not professional dazzlers, they are ordinary women. And I lust after them but not after the models in the other part of the magazine; despite the unmistakable evidence that they are real women, I can't imagine myself in bed with them, but I can imagine myself in bed with the Readers' Wives.

But that is lust. What I feel in summer walking behind a woman in a short cotton dress, her legs bare, the outline of her brassiere strap visible through the thin material, a breeze suddenly driving the skirt against her legs – that is lust. Standing near to a woman in a shop, middle-class young, a child clinging to her hand, I smell her sweat, laundered cotton, her hair – that is lust. With Sheila, quite helplessly, it is love. Lust is what I feel for all women who are attractive to me — love is what I feel only for Sheila. All that I feel for all the other women is part of that love. All that I feel for them physically; it's all there, she turns me on every time. But some of the women I know I actually like, I think of as my friends. Even at work there are women whom I like and trust. It isn't like that with Sheila. I don't like her, I don't trust her, and I never have done. I love her — there's an enormous difference.

There's a very popular illusion current about love: that once you have it, you don't need anything else. If you love your wife, you don't need *anyone* else. You have companionship, you have your meals cooked and your clothes washed and the house kept as clean as a new pin. You have passion in a well-adjusted sensible *fulfilling* way — always trying new positions and new times and new places but not being too solemn about it, making new discoveries about each other every day, sharing and rejoicing and growing closer in a lifelong duet.

It isn't like that with us. A lot of the time it's a mess. It's true that I learn new things about her every day, but none of them gives me much joy. The sex isn't always that good, either. We don't always want it at the same time. Sheila was systematic enough when she was Clifford Droylsden's secretary, but she's not systematic about sex. It can be twice and thrice a night for a fortnight, then for three weeks I hardly dare touch her. Once I couldn't get near her for six weeks, and to my mortification found myself having wet dreams.

Her one shining virtue — sometimes I think her only one — is that when after one of our hyper-active bouts I've been too tired to achieve an erection, she's always been nice about it. She can be the world's worst bitch, but she's not a ball-breaker. She is the only woman I have ever loved and, although no man can ever be certain about this until his coffin-lid is screwed down, I believe she's the only woman I ever shall love. I have often imagined myself in love, but I've always been aware that what I was doing was to paint the egg and tie a pink ribbon round it. Very pretty, but what's under the paint and the ribbon is a hard-boiled egg which sooner than you think will go bad.

When I talk about Sheila I'm talking about love, and love is far from being an entirely happy emotion – or rather state of being – but once you've experienced it, nothing less will do. There are no substitutes, or at least there are no substitutes for me. As I grow older, I look at other married couples – seeing more clearly as I grow older – and realise that there isn't any love. There are common interests, there is a matter-of-fact affection, there is, if you're very lucky, friendship, there is, above all, habit – the habit of comfort, the habit of sharing a bed, of coming home to smell a meal cooking. There's nothing wrong with any of this, but it isn't love. It's what you settle for – and love isn't what you settle for; it's what settles on you, or, rather, descends upon you, the hawk seeing its prey and dropping like a stone straight to its prey. Does the sparrow settle for the sharp beak piercing it, the claws grasping it to carry it away?

Does Sheila love me? It doesn't really matter. There have been times when I thought that she did; and if she really did then that would be a really pretty love story, a story to be set to music, a golden vase full of red roses – I would tell you this story and, long after I had told you, the memory would return to fill dull moments with scent and colour. But, remembering everything that has passed, looking soberly and clearly at all that happens between us now, I have to say it: I don't believe that Sheila loves me and I don't believe that she has ever loved anybody.

It's taken me seven years to accept this, seven years to get rid of my pride. And now I can say, without being upset at all, say it out loud sometimes when I'm alone: *As long as she's there, as long as she lets me love her, that's enough.*

I don't add *I'm happy.* Because that's a silly word to describe what I feel for her. It just isn't adequate. It doesn't include the hurt and the anger I feel, more often than not, when she's there. I have learned to control the hurt and the anger – or at least their outward manifestations. They don't diminish love; I wonder sometimes if love does not feed upon them. They do exclude happiness. Nor is it that I enjoy pain. I have enough neuroses to keep all the psychiatrists in Vienna working twenty-four hours a day for the next hundred years; but I am not a masochist. I detest pain, will go to almost any lengths to avoid even the slightest physical discomfort. I have to endure the hurt and the anger because they're part of a package deal. Happiness was no part of the package deal, though pleasure indisputably was.

And there are times when I have my doubts even about that. Kneeling over Sheila's naked body, the legs wide apart, her lips drawn back over her teeth, her breasts flattened by her recumbent position, the nipples disproportionately large, is what I experience when I touch her warm wet vulva *pleasure*?

I have to touch it, I have to stroke it, I have to find the centre of sensation, stroke, manipulate, plunge in my fingers according to her whispered, urgent instructions, always in the same order, always whispered, as if there were someone in the room who might overhear, who would stop us if they overheard her commands – *Higher, higher, gently, gently, quicker, quicker, please don't stop* – but who couldn't see, or wouldn't see. When I've had a few drinks, I have sometimes very briefly imagined this other

14

person: a very thin woman with a very small mouth, wearing a long grey dress – a light grey, a silver grey like a moonlit sky – sitting on the floor by the window, her knees drawn up to her chin, her legs concealed by the dress, sitting perfectly still, her large blue eyes wide open, but unseeing. I said that I would hold nothing back; I have not said that I would explain everything. I can neither explain that watcher in the grey dress, nor deny her reality. And I do not know whether there'll ever be a time when I'm certain that she's ceased to exist.

But all of it, all the ritual of which I've now become the high priest, isn't really pleasure. The taste of the ice-cold lager – and who the hell cares about the make? – on a summer's evening after a shower, the cool breeze through the open window: that is pleasure. The feeling which I often have in the stores on a busy Saturday afternoon, when I know without looking at the tills that business is doing well, that the money's cascading in and everyone's happy about it: that's pleasure. And, since I'm holding nothing back, my occasional trips to a Soho strip show, gloating happily over a girl's naked body, absolutely relaxed but with my groin tingling mildly, enjoying a naked female without the necessity of involvement: that is a pleasure, and the watcher in the grey dress isn't there. It would be an even greater pleasure if the girls were grown-up women, at least thirty-five but not past the menopause, obviously matrons, with sensible and matronly clothes, clothes of what Sheila calls the WVS type, not positively dowdy but not figure-revealing either, and with sensible and opaque underwear and girdles and Grippiknickers and tights – if, as I've said in another connection, they were *real women*. But real women wouldn't do it, and, even if they would, the sort of people who run strip shows aren't exactly sensitive or imaginative, nor are they dedicated students of the male psyche. They stick to the formula of smashing birds, lace and transparency, tinsel and spangles, frilly suspender belts and black stockings, because it brings the customers in, and who shall blame them?

But that is pleasure, even if for a few moments when one emerges into the street there's a faint grubbiness clinging to one like tobacco smoke on the clothes, a grubbiness which is probably based on irritation at having helped grubby, criminal Soho types to make a fat living. You buy what they have to sell, but you know that they'd just as soon sell you reefers or heroin or a gun or a bomb or even nastier things or services, and it takes three or four large whiskies to feel clean again.

And what I am saying, sitting here in my house on Sugar Hill on an August evening, only just properly cool now after a shower and a change and three lagers, is that sex with Sheila isn't pleasure. It's wonderful, the earth moves and all the rest of it, it's in my mind more perhaps than it ought to be, it's something which, when offered, I have to take. And have to take no matter if I'm tired, no matter if I'm ill, no matter if I'm on the point of leaving her, because I can't stand it any more, can't stand that smile which I glimpse when her name's mentioned. I am a man and I've worked hard to be a man; and part and parcel of being a man is that in a certain position you either kill your wife or you leave her. And none of this stops me for one moment when she makes the gesture – generally brutally simple – which indicates that she wants sex.

Which is why it has all been worth while. Which is, I suppose, what the lemmings would say, if they could speak, rushing along towards the sea, what they would say even as they drowned.

Gareth and Sharon are asleep: I sit here alone this hot

August night; the window is wide open but there's scarcely a breath of air. My glass is empty, but I don't want to get up to go to the kitchen, or else I'll stop feeling cool. The house is very quiet and Medway Close is very quiet. It generally is quiet. It was built as an exclusive development ten years ago; each of the twelve houses is detached, and none has less than half an acre. Number Eleven, my house, has two-thirds of an acre: I bought it two years ago, just as the bottom was beginning to drop out of the property market, and was able to knock four thousand off the asking price because, thanks to Clifford Droylsden, I was able to get the cash I needed; and he put in a good word for me with the building society too. The owner, an advertising whizz-kid in his thirties, was running out of whizz because he'd been let down by another purchaser and had been idiot enough to buy another house on a bridging loan; as soon as I met him I could smell the fear on him. I've often wondered what happened to him; the bottom's now dropped out of advertising also. And you can smell the fear all around the Home Counties; they've had it easy as long as they can remember and now it isn't easy any more. So I've got a five-bedroomed house with two bathrooms and a double garage and two-thirds of an acre of mature garden – he said he'd spent over a thousand having it landscaped and I believed him – for four thousand pounds under its market value, because he'd been finally forced to offer it at that. But Clifford Droylsden's loan was what clinched it.

I did want the house, and I'd always fancied Sugar Hill. But Clifford didn't help me because *I* wanted it. He helped me because Sheila wanted it – or at least because she went along with me. She would have actually preferred St George's Hill; but she knew perfectly well that Clifford – or rather his wife – wouldn't wear that. She's quite happy about Sugar Hill, but it's really the professional-man/rising-executive belt, not the stockbrokers' and pop musicians' belt as St George's Hill is. Even now, St George's Hill represents real money, the big money; they're so snooty there that the roads don't have names. I have a shrewd notion that at thirty-eight I've gone as far as I'm going to go, and I'll need more than the usual amount of luck and cunning to hang on to what I've got. Sheila still has her dreams.

Meanwhile there is Number Eleven, Medway Close — dazzling white, green tiles, shallow ranch-style roof, two bathrooms and a shower compartment, five bedrooms, four of them double-size, a separate Marley Motor House with room for two Bentleys, and the garden in good trim because the advertising whizz-kid kept it simple and concentrated on lawn and roses. The ground-floor reception rooms are parquet and the kitchen a blue delft pattern tile; the original decorations were in good order, though rather on the stark side, and so they've been redone since we came, except in two bedrooms, which Sheila will get round to any day now.

All that I've had done to the house, all that I've bought for it, has cost me about half of what it would cost my neighbours. I know who has the best goods, and who does the best job and I know who welcomes cash warmly; and I also do favours for whoever does me favours. In a perfect world there'd be a fairer and less sleazy way to survive. But this isn't a perfect world. It is all for Sheila. What she wants I give her. I only become bitter and twisted about it when occasionally she goes to London and buys from places like Harrods, with which I naturally can't do any deals. But she's not all that fond of London: it's too big, too indifferent, no one knows anyone. So that isn't really a problem; whatever she wants, I can afford it.

It's more of a struggle now to circumvent the vultures of the Inland Revenue; but as long as you're in an executive position and are handling money and saleable goods, you'll manage. Keep your mouth shut, don't trust anybody unless you've got something on them, and keep technically within the law. And then you have the parquet floor and the nice thick fitted carpeting in the bedrooms – reception-room quality, actually, but what is saved by using the less hard-wearing quality isn't worth saving. And the Sanderson wallpaper and teak and mahogany and oak and walnut, and a few genuine antiques which I picked up in the North – only a lunatic buys antiques in London and the Home Counties or indeed anywhere where there's a lot of middle-class people with more money and taste than financial sense. The house is full of stuff, full of good stuff, all mine and in good order, because I can't bear anything near me which is imperfect or doesn't function properly.

I sometimes wonder if Sheila values any of it. It gives her a kick when she's just acquired it; then she forgets it, she doesn't give a damn. She has a few, a very few, pieces of favourite jewellery – nothing fantastically expensive, but all good – that she never seems to tire of. But her dressing-table drawers are crammed with bracelets, rings, earrings and brooches which she never wears. I sometimes think that she doesn't care for *things* at all, doesn't care how she dresses, what she eats or drinks, how she lives. She is actually a good housewife, the deep-freeze is always well stocked, the place tidy, she knows how to make the daily help really help, she's good with the children, the curtains and loose covers are cleaned regularly, one never runs out of the necessities, she even knows where everything is. But she is somewhere else, she's not attached; the cat sits grooming itself, it is house-trained, it doesn't scratch you or the furniture, it is even quite affectionate, but one day it may just wander out and never return; it isn't like a dog, it isn't attached to people, only to itself.

I am still a long way from the truth. Further away than Clifford Droylsden, that's certain. He faced the facts long since. He's twenty-five years older than me, but that's nothing to do with it. My next-door neighbour, Vince Kelvedon, who earns about twelve thousand a year in a big electronics combine and who's now nearing the duodenal stage because of reorganisation higher up, isn't so far off Clifford's age but you've only got to talk to him when he's had a few whiskies to realise that he's still as full of illusions as any adolescent. Or, let's say, as the sort of adolescent I personally was. Vince, despite having been divorced once and not exactly hitting it off with his second wife, who's fifteen years younger, is apt to say, lowering his voice a couple of octaves to make it more sincere: 'Jim, you've got to *work* at marriage. It's just as difficult as building a bridge or taking out an appendix: a marriage won't look after itself . . .' Then – this was when his wife and kids were away at her mother's and I'd called in to borrow some adhesive for a very small job in the kitchen – he went on to tell me about his theories of give and take and the joys of sharing and how, over the years, a man and wife would come to understand one another, be able to communicate without speaking. And then they'd become one person, one flesh . . .

Vince is a big man, a couple of inches taller than me (and I'm five foot eleven) and twice as broad, with a lot of flesh which looks suspiciously compressed round the waist, and a large, red, rather battered face. The features are large but quite regular but they *appear* battered, rather as if he'd undergone plastic surgery and it hadn't been entirely successful. 'Fiona had to go away because her mum's not well, and I'm up to my eyes in work now,' he said. 'So what could we do? Don't mind telling you, I was looking forward to her going – whilst the cat's away and all that –' and then he gave me a theatrical wink, slow and clumsy like all his physical gestures – 'but now I'm just a bloody spare part. Lost without her. Only half of me there . . .'

That's the precise opposite of how it is with Sheila and me. I don't want to be one flesh with Sheila. Her fascination for me is and always has been that she's another flesh, a totally alien flesh. I don't want to know what she's thinking. I doubt even if I could bear to live with her if I did. I'm sure that she'd quickly stalk off into the wild wet woods if ever she had the remotest notion of what my feelings about her really are. There have been a few occasions – generally when she was absolutely, crashingly, self-admittedly in the wrong – when we've spoken our minds to each other. Or at least I've spoken my mind and she's kept her temper. But the following day we've returned to the usual stage of *détente* – no hostilities, every courtesy and a reasonable amount of goodwill and co-operation, but sticking to the rules we've worked out over five years, the first of which is *Ask no questions and you'll be told no lies*.

I've had my dreams, no less than Sheila. I've wanted the perfect woman. Because I can't see how you're going to have a marriage as perfect as my neighbour Vince claims his to be unless you have a perfect woman. Not that Vince wasn't whistling in the dark. Fiona is a dreary bitch – very earnest and always going on about the under-privileged, which Sheila, to give her credit, never has done – but she's not bad-looking and she has an Honours Degree in Economics, and she's much younger than Vince, and if Vince's firm organises as thoroughly as he fears, letting the chips fall where they may, acting in the best interests of all concerned, I wouldn't say that it was entirely impossible for her to find another man to be one flesh with. It would be true love, of course; I don't think that Vince is such an idiot that he's not aware of this, and I'm pretty sure that that's why he got pissed out of his mind that night.

My story is different. It's highly unlikely that I'll ever be interviewed about my marriage, not being the sort of person in whom the public is interested. But I would have to say, if I were being interviewed, that mine had been a lousy marriage. I suppose that a saint, if any are born these days, would conceive of it as gloriously happy. It would give him so many opportunities to suffer and to come nearer to God, so many opportunities to exercise the Christian virtue of forgiveness not ninety-nine times but a hundred times. If he were a real saint he'd consider that he'd been let down lightly; after all, being humiliated by one's wife is as nothing compared with having to kiss lepers' sores or being flayed alive and forgiving the flayers. But, needless to say, I'm not a saint, and the small and intermittent doses of Christianity administered to me in childhood have long since lost their potency.

And yet it has all been worth while. I don't want to be with her all the time. We have few tastes in common. Generally I don't like her friends and she doesn't like mine. She does meet her social obligations as my wife; I do have a certain amount of entertaining to do and there are invitations which I can't refuse, and she's never yet let me down; she knows which side her bread's buttered on. But she has a taste for low life which I don't share; I've had the suspicion now and again that she wouldn't mind drawing me in, as a quid pro quo for her doing her duty.

And that's one path I will not take; that is why at least once a week I sit in the house alone, waiting for her return, asking no questions and being told no lies.

What I have had from her, what has given my life a pattern of which I am not ashamed, what has made me a member of the human race, what has kept me from drink or worse, what has also given me a decent job and income of ten thousand, a Ford Granada, and various perquisites which add up to a tax-free three thousand extra – what I have had I cannot describe once and for all as I should describe an article at Droylsden's. It only makes sense if I begin from the beginning, if I remember what for some five years now I've been trying to forget.

For I have to understand. I must not be like the rest, lost in the fog, accepting shouted directions from the outside, accepting directions like my neighbour Vince, which infallibly take him into disaster. At thirty-eight, barring accidents, I have at least as many years again to live through. I don't want to spend any of these years in prison or a mental institution, to be discharged into, at best, a dreary routine job and a bed-sitter, with long leisure hours spent in public libraries, cinemas, strip shows when one can afford them and if the nerve hasn't been killed. Or farther down, much farther down, living on National Assistance, getting out of the habit of work, getting out of the habit of meeting people, muttering to oneself, not bothering to wash or shave, going still further until there's only the desire for oblivion, even if the oblivion tastes foul, spells out from the first mouthful a slow and nasty death. And all along the road, the hardest thing to bear, there'd be people, paid and unpaid, wanting to do good to one, and that would be worst of all.

I want to keep what I've got, I want to keep my position, I want to keep my status, I want to keep all my material possessions, and I want more of everything if I can get it. I know I can't take anything with me when I die, but I also know there won't be anywhere to take anything. There is nothing, just nothing; and I haven't noticed any of the people who say that they believe otherwise being any the less keen to pile up material goods than the rest of us. This is not original: but when one undertakes to be absolutely honest, to hold nothing back, one doesn't also undertake to be original. (Sometimes I hate the idea of going into nothing, sometimes I awake frightened in the small hours, almost afraid to fall asleep again, but of course I fall asleep again because, like us all, I don't think really that it can happen to me.)

Vince has sometimes talked about his childhood to me, and so has Fiona. In fact, they're both rather fond of looking back to those happy days, and Fiona in particular is given to feeling guilty because no matter how well Vince does as a bread-winner, their children will never be able to have such blissful security, such a super, super time as Fiona had. In fact Fiona feels guilty about it quite often, though, as she hastens to point out, this is quite illogical, since she wasn't responsible for Hitler and Stalin and Hiroshima and the Iron Curtain and global pollution and all the rest of it. But her father was a delightful slightly daffy Schools Inspector and they lived in a picture-book hamlet in the West Country, and Vince's father was an architect who lived in Hampstead. He was not quite so delightful as Fiona's father because he was a partner in a new firm which had its ups and downs, and being delightful is a more likely consequence of an assured remuneration from the public pocket than it is of having to find customers and then having to extract money from them; the law of the market is a wonderful thing but it can be very cruel. But however this may be, Vince and Fiona enjoyed their childhood. After a few Scotches, in fact, they look back at it with tears in their eyes. And so do most people, irrespective of class. Even Sheila rather enjoyed her childhood, though she's not like most people. I mean that she would even have enjoyed *my* childhood, if somehow or other we'd been exchanged in our cradles. She has, naturally, left Stoke-on-Trent far behind, just as she's totally rid herself of the Staffordshire accent, which isn't even any good for pop singers and comedians.

Sheila, though, isn't affected by the world around her. She makes the best of it, thinks her own thoughts, and bides her time. 'She's a deep bugger, that one,' her mother has often said to me. 'Never could tell what went on in her head even when she was little. Cyril now, it's all straight out with Cyril –' and then she talks about Cyril, her pride and joy, the clever one, who was a wild colonial boy when he was younger but who came to his senses and now is a lecturer at a college of education in Yorkshire and a bigger bore you have never met. (With the possible exception of Bruce, Sheila's half-brother, who's a sales rep in the Sheffield area; but he is another story.) Sheila smiles at those moments and goes on being a deep bugger; she has heard it all before.

I have built up a picture of her childhood over the years. Her father was killed in Burma, but they managed quite well. 'We did better when the sod was called up than before he went away,' Sheila's mother has said more than once. I suppose that things were better then in a way; the part of Stoke-on-Trent where she spent her childhood was pretty horrible but everyone knew each other, and Sheila's grandparents and two aunts and an uncle lived nearby. And there were cousins and family friends and family businesses; everybody in the Potteries was related to everybody else or had worked with or for them: there

25

weren't really any strangers or all that many immigrants. It wasn't my cup of tea, because it was so hideous, but she could have done worse.

But I did not enjoy my childhood. I was not ill treated; I was always well dressed and well fed and, indeed, rather spoiled, being an only child. And being good-looking, with large blue eyes and fair curly hair and regular features; the hair darkened into mousy brown when I was two but I still was good-looking. It helps a great deal in the battle of life, particularly if you have an open expression and keep your eyes fixed upon the face of the person to whom you're talking.

The town where I lived was then an independent urban district some five miles west of Wigan. My father was the office manager for a middle-sized builder's firm. He had a staff of one typist; I suppose that these days he'd have a deputy and half a dozen typists all falling over each other. He had a reasonable salary – three hundred a year in 1939 – but in the light of what I know now he was worth at least twice that to them. I suppose that he had the opportunity to make a bit on the side, but I don't believe that he availed himself very much of the opportunity, and his boss, an inspired crook himself, was glad of it but rather despised him for being such a fool. My father did have a fairish School Certificate – one Distinction, three Credits, and three Passes – but there he had stopped. I don't really know anything about his job, because he never talked about it; I'm sure that, as with most people, it bored him stiff. He was a tall, thin man who went grey in his early thirties; he didn't talk much, had few interests beyond thrillers and the cinema, and few friends. He smoked Woodbines – twenty a day, no more, no less – and he brewed his own beer and occasionally would sit in his favourite chair to the right of the fireplace reading thrillers or listening to the radio; and, I now realise, getting gently pissed.

Which I am now, rising to look through the open window at the rose bushes at the bottom of the garden, lemon-yellow, creamy white, scarlet, and the pale blue and violet lobelia next to them, and the lavender bushes near the window on the right and the apricot-coloured torch lilies on the left; I can smell the lavender now. And then I look away from the window: it's growing darker and the silver birches at the bottom of the garden, behind the rose bushes, appear faintly luminous. I'm not the world's greatest gardener, but merely to look at my garden gives me continuing pleasure, only marred by the reflection that this is what I do instead of reading thrillers, that I am getting gently pissed just like my father, that just like my father I know where to stop, but I am not going to stop just yet but am going to go into the kitchen and take out another can of lager from the huge black refrigerator – almost as tall as me, an experimental model which I got at one-third of the retail price because no one in this area likes black refrigerators – and I'm going to sit down at the long pitchpine table, and look at the blue formica-topped kitchen units and, just to give myself something to think about, consider changing them for pine-topped units; Sheila would like that. And so I take out the can of lager, rip off the tab under the cover of a tea-towel, and pour it into the glass carefully to keep the froth down.

And all this is dodging the issue. I have promised to go to the old battlefield, back to where I first received my wound. Now in a sense being victorious, now literally living on a hill, my wound healed, why should I revisit that desolate area, that dark tangle of pain and humiliation? There are no coach-trips there, no trains running,

27

no refreshment available on the way; I shall go alone, slowly and laboriously.

It can't be put off any longer. To think about Sugar Hill or Droylsden's or even Sheila is the equivalent of sharpening pencils which don't need to be sharpened, of having yet another cup of coffee, of asking for a set of figures to be looked up which one doesn't really need, of discovering that the one tool which one hasn't got is the only one with which to do the job properly. And if I put this job off any longer, then for want of a nail the kingdom will be lost. Maybe it isn't much of a kingdom when I compare it with the kingdoms of others. But it's the only kingdom I have and the only kingdom I'm ever likely to have.

So that when I think of that special look on people's faces in the Sheila Seathwaite country, I swallow any anger. I have to perceive my hurt as a minor hurt, a graze, a scratch. The big wound is healed. And if it is to stay healed, if it is not to reopen and turn septic and stinking, I have to return to the battlefield, the place where the wound was inflicted. I have to remember the person who inflicted it – and not with bitterness or hatred, but with absolute clarity, *holding nothing back.*

My father wasn't called up, because he had a bronchial condition and a weak heart. The War didn't make much difference to the town anyway. It was hardly worth bombing, even if the Germans had known of its existence. It was a mining town with a couple of cotton mills and it seemed in that part of the valley to rain most of the time, which is of course why the mills were there in the first place, since cotton threads snap in a dry atmosphere. There was one straggling main street, a cinema, a dance-hall, two Italian cafés, ten pubs, twelve working-men's clubs, a lot of little shops, and the Co-op Emporium. There was a café in the Co-op Emporium which had table-cloths and middle-aged waitresses and which was the only place where you could get a reasonable facsimile of a proper meal. The houses were mostly Accrington brick terrace houses built in the 1900s – the brick had once been a cheerful but not gaudy yellow; now it was black with yellow in the back-ground, the colour of a heavy bruise. There were two council estates on the southern verge of the town, and a newish estate – all semi-detached red brick – to the north. This estate was where we lived. It stood higher than the council estate, about a mile and a half from the centre, the centre being the Town Hall and Library, which were near the railway station at the south end of the main street. They also were built in the 1900s: the Town Hall was sham Gothic and narrow in proportion to its height, with a narrow and lofty entrance hall, and the windows were high and narrow and pointed at the top; and the Library, separated from it by the Spinner's Arms, a large pub built in the 1920s which looked more like a bank than a pub, was in the same style as the pub, with the addition of an over-large portico with six rather thin pillars, which seemed to have been added as an afterthought to distinguish it from the pub. It was actually a Carnegie Library and, like most Carnegie Libraries, too big for the town. Both buildings, like the rest of the buildings in the town, were almost jet black. And even our estate was already grubby.

My father came from Manchester, like my mother. Soon after they'd married, he'd lost his job – he was the senior clerk in a firm of exporters who suddenly found themselves with nothing to export – and had heard of the job at the builder's through my Uncle Sidney, who had had some business dealings in the town, but who lived in Wilmslow himself in a large detached house. Uncle Sidney is part of my story, in fact it would have been a very different story without him.

There is very little to be said about our house: it was a very plain red-brick semi-detached house built in 1934, with a small front and back garden with just enough room for a decent show of flowers and some vegetables in the strip at the side. There was even a crab-apple tree and a tiny hut where my father kept his tools and lawn-mower – which was of course hand-drawn. There was no garage; at the time the house was built it wasn't presumed that the kind of person who would buy it would be able to afford a car. But my father's Austin Seven saloon was perfectly safe parked outside and always started the first time no matter what the weather. I wouldn't mind having it now: it was a 1936 blue Austin Ruby saloon and my father maintained it himself and it never gave him any trouble because the design was so simple – in fact so primitive – that there was nothing much to go wrong with it.

Inside there was a tiny kitchen, a living-room (which my mother called the lounge), and a sitting-room. Upstairs there was a bathroom and WC, two medium-sized rooms, and a room which would only just accommodate a single bed. The water was heated by a fire-back boiler; if you wanted hot water the fire had to be lighted even in summer. There was no heat upstairs at all. But in 1939, my father, who with all his faults wasn't mean, bought two electric fires cheap for the bedrooms and a paraffin heater for the bathroom.

And now I begin. Now I face it. Now I exhume what I buried deep down when I left Lancashire. It has never come out except in dreams and sometimes when drunk. I have not only buried the memory, I have put up no gravestone, I have built a town over the grave, a *white* town, a *shining* town, a *clean* town, with broad streets with plane trees and cypresses planted alongside them, with a great square in the centre with seats and flowerbeds and fountains and more plane trees and cypresses; and in that town the houses are in the town itself, in amongst the shops and restaurants and pubs, and the town smells of roasting coffee and wine and malt and cologne, and as the girls in their summer dresses walk around the square – no cars allowed, the square is where you sit in the sunshine, where you promenade in your new clothes – you can see their bodies moving in a slightly different rhythm from their dresses, a counterpoint of fresh firm flesh and clean flimsy fabric. And in the houses – the *white* houses, the *shining* houses, the *clean* houses – the furniture is all new, new but *good, solid,* a pleasure to touch as well as a pleasure to look at; and nothing in those houses is cheap or ugly or badly designed, and they eat fresh meat and fish and seafood and salads in season and fresh fruit and cheese for dessert, and they dress casually but their clothes are laundered and regularly dry-cleaned and they wouldn't be seen dead in dirty second-hand trendy kit, and everyone washes their hair every day. And that is another of the smells in my town: clean hair and clean bodies and clean clothes – clean but not disinfected or deodorised, because disinfectants and deodorants are for urinals and WCs, not people.

My town has been a long time building and perhaps never will be complete; there is always something fresh to add, new trees and flowers to be planted, festivals and carnivals to be arranged and fireworks in the park which surrounds the town. There is no poverty there, no accidents, no ill-health unless you count slight hangovers and sexual fatigue; the poor and the ugly and the sick are not forbidden to enter but they simply don't come to live there. To be quite frank about it, their faces wouldn't fit. In my town we are good neighbours, always ready to lend a cup of sugar or a packet of tea, ready even to baby-sit or lend a car or administer a stiff drink and sympathy; we are not poor or ugly or sick but we are human, and lose jobs or lovers or husbands or wives or for no reason are depressed, not suicidally, but enough to want company. But we do not want to do good, we don't lie awake at night worrying about injustice, and no demonstrations are allowed in the town. We wish everyone well, we quarrel with nobody; but we only care about ourselves and our families and friends. The town stands on a hill and no floods or dirt or fog can reach us and we're well out of the flight path of the jets and no juggernauts are allowed near the town.

The grave is deep underneath it; I know the exact spot in the centre of the town square under the fountain – white Carrara marble with a quartet of nymphs surrounded by dolphins, coins glittering on the bottom of the basin through the clear water. Blow up the fountain, dig deep into the chalky earth; and this is to carry the image ridiculously far, for once I begin to dig, once I begin to remember what all these years I have forgotten, it is as if the town had never existed. There is only the sitting-room one September afternoon in 1944 back in that small town in Lancashire, that small town where every other person was poor or ugly or sick and you could taste the dirt in the air and it always seemed to be raining.

The suite in the sitting-room was real leather with brass studs. There was a two-seater sofa and two arm-chairs; the seats were unusually deep and the backs unusually thick, but the dimensions always seemed to me smaller than they should have been. There was a dark oak drop-side table by the front window, with spiral legs, and a small dark oak sideboard and a small dark oak coffee-table. There was a small circular table near the side window with a large blue vase with yellow and orange chrysanthemums in it. Even then they were not a flower I liked – too large, too garish, too somehow flashy, and with no scent. But if they had had a scent it would have been killed by the smell of Uncle Sidney's cheroot. He always smoked Burmese cheroots, very tightly-packed and solid-looking with an aroma totally different from Havana or Jamaican, acrid, faintly spicy, almost on the verge of the edible, approaching the perfumed but missing it, and somehow managing to be aphrodisiac. Could I sense this at seven years of age? Yes, I could. This is what is in the grave, this is what I have chosen to forget, and this is what I am going to remember now no matter what it does to me.

There are other things to remember and they are all important. For once it was not raining. The sky outside was blue, a pale washed-out blue, but not grey and black. The sun was behind the clouds but it was at least discernible. It wasn't cold, but there was a roaring fire. The fireplace was in a checkerboard pattern of red and black with a dark oak surround and mantelpiece with a large gilt mirror above it. There was my parents' wedding-group on the mantelpiece in a silver frame. Uncle Sidney was there next to my father, being his best man.

When I looked at the wedding photo – and this is one of my few memories before the age of five – I always had to look hard to identify my Uncle Sidney. He was at that time a year older than my father, which would have made him twenty-six. He was as thin as my father, both in the body and in the face. He was rather better-looking than my father, with a thin high-bridged nose and dark well-marked eyebrows and a small but full mouth and a cleft chin, and his hair was fair and curly. My father's hair was both lank and sparse and his features slightly askew; the left eye was set at a slightly different level from the other, and the right ear was a fraction larger than the left, and his nose, whilst the same shape as my Uncle Sidney's, had a deflected septum which made it appear slightly hooked. It wasn't that he was ugly; but when you saw him side by side with my Uncle Sidney it was as if the intention had been to create a handsome man and he had been the first attempt, the rough draft. Uncle Sidney was the finished job, the display model.

What was also rather unfair was that though they were the same height and build and both were wearing hired morning-suits with carnations in the buttonhole, Uncle Sidney looked smarter than my father. His suit hung better, the creases were sharper, his shirt whiter, his shoes shinier. And yet when you looked closer there wasn't any difference. Item by item their clothes were identical: the same material, the same cut, in the same condition. It was a matter of what they added up to.

In the ten years which had passed since my parents' wedding, Uncle Sidney had put on a little weight and added a few lines to his face. But the sort of clothes which he wore – in his own words, from a funny little Yid in Dewsbury who wasted no money on fancy premises or advertising but was an angel with the shears – did more than disguise it, in fact made him appear both imposing and thoroughly at ease. Nothing changes: the secret, then as now, was the finest material and no skimping. That day he wore a dark blue double-breasted pin-stripe, a white silk collar-attached shirt with a gold tie-pin, a maroon-and-blue Paisley pattern silk tie, maroon silk socks, and black casuals, a kind of shoe you very rarely saw those days.

Come to that, you didn't very often see collar-attached shirts, except the sports variety. What was more, his had double cuffs and he wore gold cufflinks with them. He had of course his Disabled Ex-Serviceman badge in his buttonhole; he had been invalided out of the Army after Dunkirk with a shattered left kneecap, which left him with a slight limp which didn't noticeably cramp his style but which nipped in the bud nasty cracks about fit men of military age making a fortune whilst Our Lads fought and bled. My father, who was given to striding from place to place briskly and springily, was the one who was the target for such remarks, and he didn't have a Disabled Serviceman's badge or hair-raising stories of his experiences at Dunkirk and the long struggle to save his leg — *Not that I'm not grateful, mind you, but by God I wouldn't like to go through it again* . . .

The extraordinary thing about Uncle Sidney was the difference he made to the atmosphere of the house. It wasn't just the smell of his Burmese cheroots or his expensive shaving-soap or his Eau-de-Portugal hair-tonic; he seemed somehow to abolish the mundane smells, to kill the smell of washing soda, carbolic, fish, dust in the carpets, blacklead, the slight mustiness of the sitting-room. And the grey-and-white flowered paper in the sitting-room, the brown-and-grey Wilton carpet, the chocolate-brown (plain chocolate, not milk) velvet curtains, seemed to acquire new colour, the dark furniture to have an extra gleam. Neither my mother nor my father had any colour sense, but when Uncle Sidney was in the house it was as if they had, or as if one could see the colours which must have been in their minds when they selected the wallpaper and carpet and curtains and furniture.

All this is relevant. I must miss none of it. If I leave anything out, even those white five-petalled flowers of no

35

known species on the wallpaper, the hexagonal pattern on the carpet, then I shall be running away, I shall be allowing that Lancashire town to vanish into the mist and the rain, I shall be commanding the sun to shine, I shall be rebuilding my shining town.

My Uncle Sidney is drinking tea from a Royal Doulton cup, part of our best tea-service, white with a gold interior, only brought out for his visits and for funerals and christenings and weddings. I still have that set packed away in the loft, never yet used by me. He drinks tea without milk or sugar, though he would prefer a slice of lemon with it. His hair is gleaming, his gold tie-pin is gleaming, his heavy gold signet-ring is gleaming, his gold wrist-watch is gleaming, the fair hairs on the back of his hands are gleaming. I am sitting on the sofa beside my Uncle Sidney, drinking tea which is half milk with three teaspoonfuls of sugar. I am wearing a grey home-knitted jersey, brown tweed shorts which almost cover my knees, grey stockings, and black boots. The brand name on the boot-tags is Little Gent; I keep tucking them into the boots so that they won't show, but they always pop out again. The leather of the sofa was cold at first but now it's warm.

My mother is sitting in the armchair by the fireplace. She was thirty-three years old then; as far as I can judge from old photos she didn't look it. I don't mean that thirty-three is a great age; I mean that without benefit of face-lifts and at a time when make-up was rather hit-or-miss she had an almost flawless skin and a slim figure and hadn't, like the overwhelming majority of women in the town, said goodbye to her youth once she was married. She had been a hairdresser before she was married and her hair was always clean and gleaming and she didn't go in for the stiff lacquered impossibly regular permanent waves of that era. She had black hair, worn long, blue eyes, and an expression which alternated between extreme animation and a pouting sulkiness. She was, at the moment I was drinking my tea, looking rather sulky, the full lips pouting like a baby's. She kept licking her lips. Her lips seemed more heavily painted than usual; she favoured a dark shade of red, and when a cloud passed across the sun her mouth for a moment seemed almost black.

She was wearing a matching jacket and skirt of a plum-coloured barathea and a low-necked shirt-style pink rayon blouse, the collar worn outside the jacket; she was fiddling with the buttons and I remember, as if it was yesterday, those rather stubby fingers with the long red finger-nails – dark red like her lipstick – as if about to unfasten the pink fabric-covered buttons but never quite getting round to it. And I remember glancing at my Uncle Sidney and noticing beads of sweat on his forehead.

'Are you hot, Uncle Sidney?' I asked.

He took the white silk handkerchief – not folded in two neat triangles, but carelessly thrust into his breast pocket in such a way as to make it plain it was silk – and dabbed his brow. 'Your mother keeps a good fire,' he said in his rather hoarse voice from which almost all traces of Lancashire had been expunged.

My mother smiled, but didn't say anything. The shoulders of her jacket were padded to give the square military look which the moronic designers of the time thought that women hankered for; but on her it was as if she was somehow in masquerade, the heroine who has borrowed the hussar's jacket and who looks all the more feminine in it.

Uncle Sidney stood up, took his jacket off, and neatly folded it over the back of the other chair.

'Make yourself at home,' my mother said. 'Take your

shoes off and put your feet up whilst you're about it.' The intimate, conspiratorial tone in which she spoke seemed to belong to a different set of words, the meaning of which I couldn't even begin to guess at.

'Little pitchers,' said my uncle. I noticed that he was wearing a narrow black leather belt and that the trousers had belt-loops; this again was very rare at that period. He glanced out of the window. 'Not a bad day.'

'What do you mean, Uncle Sidney?' I asked him.

'What do I mean by what?' There was something odd about his trousers, something I didn't understand.

'Little pitchers. What do you mean by little pitchers?'

'It's a saying,' my uncle said. 'Just a saying.' He sat down again.

My mother had long legs with slender ankles but well muscled; a little more muscle and they would have been too heavy, but as it was, they were perfect. She was wearing fully-fashioned flesh-coloured nylons – my uncle had in fact brought them for her on his last visit – and her skirt only just covered her knees.

'I think that your uncle's got something for you,' my mother said. She unfastened the top button of her blouse, her eyes on my uncle's waistline.

'I've always got something for Sonny,' my uncle said. He ruffled my hair; his hand was hot and moist. He pulled a sweets ration book and five shillings out of his pocket. I'd never had so much money before; in 1944 five pounds a week was still a living wage. 'Mum's the word,' he said. 'Don't tell anyone, not even your father. Else I'll go to prison.'

My mother fastened the top button of her blouse again. As she did so she momentarily revealed half an inch of white brassiere. I wouldn't have had a name for the garment at that age; what I did know was that something had been revealed which ought not to have been revealed and a promise had been made which ought not to have been made. My father used to buy me my sweets on Saturday and only on Saturday; I had a sudden mental picture of myself half running alongside him, my hand on his arm, and felt uneasy. Not guilty precisely; though that was on its way. But as if I had somehow let him down.

'Well, what do you say?' my mother asked me sharply. She crossed her legs, then for a second had trouble with her skirt. I had a glimpse of her stocking-tops, the metal and cloth of her suspender fastener, the white lace edging of her blue knickers. Then her knees were together, her hands round her knees. The wound had been inflicted. Not a battle wound, when now I consider the circumstances of its infliction. I was too young to be a soldier, too young for any battle except Cowboys and Indians, Cops and Robbers, Roundheads and Cavaliers, mock battles with blunted arrows and cap guns and wooden swords and hobby-horses. The wound was a real one, the bullet was real, the sniper hadn't been aiming at me, but that didn't stop the bullet from hurting me, that wouldn't make the wound any the less ugly or crippling.

I have to go further. Never mind my father. Never mind my uncle. My story is about me. This is where it starts. And this is where I'd like to end it. I said: 'Thank you very much, Uncle Sidney,' but didn't move. I was too interested in looking at his trousers. They seemed to have changed shape, and he was in an attitude of discomfort which was contradicted by the expression in his eyes, which I identified, as far as I could identify it, as pure greed. He became aware of me looking at him, stubbed out his cheroot, took his jacket away from the chair, put it over his lap, and took out the packet of cheroots.

'Why don't you go out and buy some sweeties?' my mother asked.

I should have stayed. I should have asked my mother to keep the five shillings for me. I should have pretended I was ill. It would have been easy enough; my not wanting to go out to spend the five shillings (a great sum then) would have been cast-iron evidence that I wasn't malingering, young though I was. But I took the money and ran out. When I was at the front door – the tiny hall was next to the sitting-room – I heard Uncle Sidney laugh.

'Christ,' he said in a low voice, 'I nearly came.'

'Quiet,' my mother said. 'Be quiet, you fool!'

I went out, closing the door very quietly, and walked slowly down the asphalt path, scuffing my feet. I bent down to tuck the Little Gent tags inside my boots, then gave that up. The road was very quiet; the only car there was my Uncle Sidney's maroon Rover Sixteen Sportsman's Saloon. My father cleaned and polished the Austin every Sunday, but it never shone as richly as the Rover.

The road was more in the nature of a track; like a lot of roads on private estates at that period it had never been made up, but since there was only one other car-owner on the road, an insurance agent who ran a Morris Eight, no one was inclined to bother. In fact, the general feeling was that the bumpiness of the road – drivers threaded their way between the bumps at a snail's-pace – made it safer for the children. Now residents' associations have ramps built, which cost money and don't slow cars down half as well.

I'm still dodging the issue. I walked slowly along the road, looking down at the valley below with the pall of smoke above the bruise-black-and-yellow brick of the houses, the sound of machinery from the mills being part of the quiet, a few lorries trundling along the main street. It wasn't exactly a town in which the pleasure principle was predominant. I don't think that there was one inhabitant who didn't work; when they retired, it was because they were worn out, and they haunted the Public Library reading-rooms and the Veterans' Shelter in the King George the Fifth Park, shuffling and dingy, smelling of snuff and urine and black shag tobacco. (Although at that time this would only apply to a minority; in 1944 you had to be very old and decrepit and stupid indeed not to be able to get some kind of job.)

Once I was out of sight of our house and in sight of the newsagent's in the next street, I began to think of what I would buy with the five shillings which Uncle Sidney had given me. Half-crowns were very satisfactory coins; they always seemed much more than one-fifth more valuable than florins. I could buy not only some sweets, I realised, but a Dinky Toy besides. Or, better still, two Tootsie Toys. I liked the Tootsie Toys, which were American, rather better than the Dinky Toys. There was a very attractive sedanca de ville based, I think, on a Graham-Paige, and a La Salle coupé; they'd been there as long as I could remember and Jock Finnart, the proprietor, had forgotten about them. In fact, when I went into the shop to ask for them, he couldn't find them, and had to search in the back for them.

Finnart's shop was one of a small arcade comprising a hairdresser, a butcher, a fishmonger, a greengrocer, a fish-and-chip shop, and an off-licence shop which was also a general stores. He was a small man in his forties with a lilting accent which everyone assumed was Welsh but was in fact Highland; his wife Ada came from the town, and they had been married for twenty years but had had no children. I don't quite know how or why he'd come to

Lancashire, but he told me once that all that there was in the Highlands was scenery and you can't eat scenery.

'Is it that you've come into a fortune, then?' he asked me as he brought out the Tootsie Toys.

'My Uncle Sidney gave me some money.' Even as I spoke, I felt that I had no business to tell him.

Finnart looked at me fixedly. He had short sandy hair parted dead centre and always plastered down with fixative; his pale blue eyes did not smile, but his mouth was always smiling, showing china-white false teeth. 'Now isn't that the splendid thing! What a kind man Uncle Sidney is to be sure!'

His wife, a small thin woman, with a round face oddly similar to her husband's in colouring and expression, had suddenly appeared in the shop with a pint mug of tea. She seemed to have heard our conversation.

'Uncle Sidney is a very kind man, isn't he, love?' she said to me. 'And what a lovely car he has and such lovely clothes.'

'He knows how to make his petrol spin out,' Jock said.

'Your Dad'll be pleased to see him,' Jock's wife said. 'Always an event when your Uncle Sidney comes to see you, isn't it, love?'

'I like my Uncle Sidney,' I said lamely. 'I'll have a bar of milk chocolate, please. And a quarter of pear-drops.'

'No milk, only blended. It's nearly as good.' He weighed out the pear-drops: their sharp smell cut through the smell of hot tea and newsprint and tobacco. The shop, like most newsagents', made its main profits from tobacco, sweets, ice-cream, stationery and so on; the newspapers and magazines got people into the shop. Finnart was a good shopkeeper, I was aware even then, though he was a horrible man. I liked his shop because it was clean and tidy and well arranged; there were never any flyblown displays or out-of-date advertisements and even the notices which he displayed for, I think, threepence a week were neatly arranged on a proper notice-board outside, instead of being stuck inside the window. And whatever one might want in the way of stationery was always in stock, even in 1944. Games too; he even had Monopoly and Totopoly and backgammon sets in stock. Another thing always in stock was gossip; without my realising it, I brought him in a fresh supply that day.

I took the Tootsie Toys and the chocolate and pear-drops and ran out of the shop. Suddenly I wasn't happy to be there, I didn't want to browse amongst the stock as I usually did, I didn't even want a comic. Outside I looked at the half-crown which I had in my hand and for no reason wanted to throw it down the grating. I even wanted to throw away the Tootsie Toys and the sweets. The wound was beginning to smart. Since then I have learned from men who have actually been in battle that even the worst wounds don't hurt at the time. There's a sudden blow, a shock, then nothing is felt at all. And not till later comes the pain.

I was of course wildly ignorant of the facts of life. I was a rather prudish child, and sex wasn't something which my father and mother ever talked about. They weren't especially mealy-mouthed and they weren't above the occasional bawdy joke, but as far as they were concerned it was a subject not to be talked about in front of the children. My little schoolmates used to have surreptitious conversations about it, but for some reason I was rarely included in these conversations. And when I was I couldn't connect what they'd seen horses and bulls doing with whatever it was that human beings did. Much less could I connect it with my treasured, guilty, secret pleasure, discovered by accident, indulged in only in the bathroom and bed, a pleasure unlike all other pleasures, as if stolen from the adult world.

And now I could, standing on that windswept arcade at the top of a hill, with the sun shining palely but with winter in the air, with a paper carrier-bag in my hand containing the pear-drops and the chocolate and the Tootsie Toys. The worst of it was that I hadn't wanted to look at what my mother had momentarily but so deliberately revealed, that one part of me had found it ugly and frightening. The curious thing is that ever since then, unlike most men of my age-group, I've never really been turned on by stockings and suspenders. I don't suppose that I'd look away from any leg-show involving them, but the garments themselves haven't been what has interested me, only what was inside them.

And this was the wound. What, even at the age of seven, I desired was forbidden. No one had to tell me. It was not only forbidden but entangled with betrayal. At the same time I knew that I would continue to be painfully – that is the right word – interested in it.

I walked slowly down the street to my home. It would have been just five o'clock; I heard the Town Hall clock striking far away, an odd carillon like a big pot cracking sharply, the bark of a huge sheepdog. I wished that I had bought some comics, but I didn't want to return to Finnart's.

When I tried to open the door, the lock was on the sneck. I rang the bell once, twice, three times, and then began to panic. Uncle Sidney's car was still there, but there was no one in the sitting-room. I suddenly felt an unreasoning fear of being abandoned, cast off as a punishment. There was no doubt by now that I deserved punishment, but I still couldn't have said precisely why.

Then I heard the sneck click down and my mother

opened the door. She was flushed and smelled of soap and powder and violets. Violets – not a scent one comes across very often these days, too sweet, too cloying for my taste even then.

'You look cold,' she said. 'Did you get your sweets?'

I nodded. I didn't want to speak to her. I didn't want to speak to anybody.

She held out her hand for the carrier-bag. 'I'll keep them for you.' She winked. 'Don't tell Dad. He thinks you're spoiled as it is.'

'Where's Uncle Sidney?' I asked. 'Has he gone?'

'Thickhead! Can't you see his car's still outside? Where do you think he is?' She seemed somehow larger, more curved, more feminine, the cat that had got at the cream.

There was the sound of the WC flushing from upstairs and Uncle Sidney came down, rubbing his hands together nervously. 'Hullo, Sonny. Did you get your sweeties?' He ruffled my hair. He seemed somehow subdued, not quite the man he was. The lines at the corners of his eyes and on his forehead and from his nostrils to the corners of his mouth seemed not as they had been, almost cosmetic, as if deliberately applied to indicate maturity, but now seemed as if savagely scored with a sharp instrument to remind him that he wasn't really young any longer. The glitter, the braggadocio, were dimmed. He went into the sitting-room, followed by my mother, and warmed his hands by the fire.

'I have to go to Scotland for a while, Valerie,' he said. 'I may be there quite a bit.' He straightened up, took out a Burmese cheroot and lit it. Warming his hands and lighting the cheroot seemed to switch something on which had been switched off before: the glitter and the braggadocio were back at full strength. 'Wish I could persuade old Len to come with me,' he said. 'God, now's the time to get a footing: now's the time to set up a business. He'll get nowhere with that bloody jerry-builder boss of his.'

My mother had sat down. Her skirt seemed now to have lengthened by three or four inches so that it was amply covering her knees. 'There's no telling him,' she said. 'Don't you think he's had plenty of offers?'

My uncle began to stride up and down the room, as if he could no longer restrain his energy. 'Of course he has!' he shouted. 'They can see him running that bloody business virtually single-handed, working all hours that God sends, with no bloody overtime because he's the office manager, can't they? And what does his boss do? Makes contacts in the bloody pubs and clubs and hotels, spends the bloody profits and pretends he's a big businessman. He wouldn't last for five minutes without Len.'

'Who wouldn't?' asked my father as he came into the room, bent down and kissed my mother on the cheek, and squeezed me by the shoulders.

'Your bloody boss wouldn't. Everybody knows what a lazy useless sod he is.'

'He'd do without me before I could do without him,' my father said, slumping into the armchair nearest the sofa. He searched through his pockets and brought out a packet of Woodbines.

'Have a proper smoke,' my uncle said, offering him the packet of cheroots.

My father shook his head. 'They taste like a hair-dresser's shop to me.' He lit his Woodbine and, as everyone used to do then, inhaled the smoke deep into his lungs and exhaled it through his nose. He fiddled with his shirt-collar and tie, then stopped, seeing my mother frown at him. When he came home he invariably loosened his tie and collar and took them off with the tie still knotted, and then took off his jacket. It was a habit of his which never failed to irritate my mother; she said it was common.

My father was wearing his usual working suit, a navy blue serge three-piece which had cost him fifty shillings five years ago. The shirt was blue striped and he wore a dark blue striped tie with it. His socks were navy-blue and his shoes black and broad-fitting. My mother put out a clean shirt and tie for him every morning, or otherwise he would have worn the same ones until they fell to pieces. It wasn't that he was dirty; he simply didn't care what he wore.

My Uncle Sidney looked at him and frowned, then went into the hall – or rather the very small space at the bottom of the stairs – and came back with a pigskin briefcase. He took out a bottle of Haig whisky. 'Get some glasses, Val, will you?' he asked my mother.

Surprisingly, for I'd never seen her go there before except to dust it, she went to the china cabinet and brought out three small glasses. I remember now that they were cut glass with a diamond pattern and too small for whisky glasses. But whisky – or any other spirit – was virtually never drunk in our house except at Christmas and other special occasions.

My Uncle Sidney opened the bottle. 'Val?'

'Please,' my mother said. 'It's a medicine, after all.'

'Len? Just the stuff after a hard day.'

'I don't mind if I do,' my father said. He wasn't using the radio catchphrase of the time, because he didn't speak in the obligatory parody-drunk form, slurring the words. It was how he always accepted a drink; this again never failed to irritate my mother and I saw her frowning again.

'Here's to us,' said my uncle, raising his glass. 'And here's to you changing your job, Len, before it's too bloody late. Do you know why I'm going to Scotland? Because I know some chaps there who've got some money.

There's a lot around, and there's a lot of stuff now can be bought cheap.'

'Scotland's a funny place to go for brass,' my father said. *Brass* meaning money was not a word he often used; I think that for him to do so was an indication that he didn't take my uncle very seriously.

'Sidney knows what he's doing,' my mother said sharply.

'I hope he does,' my father said and sipped his whisky placidly. Even with his collar and tie obviously irritating him, he was the most relaxed person I've ever met. Uncle Sidney seemed to be moving fast, hurrying to a fixed goal, even when sitting still.

'You're just like bloody Emma,' my uncle said. 'You want to stay put; you don't like taking risks. God, that's the breath of life to me.'

'Slow and sure wins the race,' my father said. He lit another Woodbine. 'How is Emma?'

'As always,' my uncle said. 'Everything passes over her head. As long as she's got the chapel and the kids she's happy as Harry.'

My Aunt Emma was a large billowy blonde who had been one of my mother's bridesmaids. They'd worked in the same hairdresser's salon. Slow-moving and slow-speaking, nothing fazed Emma; if she had an objection to make, she made it, and then forgot about it. They had sons of three and four, Malcolm and Trevor, who were too young to be of any use as playmates to me, and whom I didn't in any case see very often. Aunt Emma had religion, though mildly; Uncle Sidney, like my father, didn't have it at all, but he didn't put any obstacles in her way. He was, I can see now, pushing, ruthless, devious, greedy, and completely amoral; but he wasn't intolerant. I do not hate him now, and I did not hate him then.

There was a moment of silence after my uncle had

spoken; my father smoked his Woodbine and sipped his whisky, a faraway look in his eye, and I seem to remember, but am not absolutely sure, that my Uncle Sidney kept looking at my mother's legs. My mother broke the silence, which was fast becoming an awkward one.

'I'll have to think about tea,' she said, and rose. Then I saw that her skirt was indeed three or four inches longer, that it was neither the same skirt nor the same jacket, that the material was the same, but that the colour was nearer scarlet than plum. Then I looked again and her blouse was white, not pink, and I was seized by a strange hot excitement, half a tingling sensation, half nausea. I looked away from her quickly and thought of the La Salle coupé and the Graham-Paige sedanca de ville – opulence and blue skies, palm-trees and cactus, Cary Grant and Veronica Lake, guns and Humphrey Bogart, the taste of Spam, which at seven I rather liked, and the taste of a pork pie (made from a can of American pork which Uncle Sidney brought us last Christmas) which I had liked still more.

'You're going out with me,' Uncle Sidney said. 'There's a place in Manchester run by a mate of mine . . .' He winked. 'Real steak, not the kind that goes *Heehaw Heehaw*. Wine from France, the real stuff.' He smacked his lips. 'Auntie Ada'll look after Sonny. I'll give her a ten-bob note and she'll be delighted.'

'She might be going out,' my father said.

'For Christ's sake, how do you know until you ask her? Auntie Ada never goes out. She sits in listening to the the radio.' *Radio* was very much the *in* word then; most people still said *wireless*. My uncle moved quickly to the door. 'I'll tootle over and ask her.'

My Auntie Ada was in fact my mother's aunt, a widow who lived in a small cottage, originally a farm cottage, about half a mile away. Her husband had been employed in the Rates Department at the Town Hall; he had died before I was born. She was a tall woman with a straight back, described always as well-spoken. She had a pension from the Council and did odd dressmaking jobs; she had in fact been a dressmaker before her marriage. She'd had no children, but not out of choice; she genuinely did love children and they loved her. I wish to God I had someone like her living near me now.

He did tootle over and ask her, and she came. My father, grumbling in an ineffective sort of way, was made to put on his best suit – a pinhead pattern dark grey worsted – and a clean white shirt and the maroon silk tie my mother had given him for Christmas, with maroon silk socks to match and a clean white handkerchief for his breast pocket. My mother folded it for him with four small triangles showing, but even before he got out of the house he had managed to make it disappear into the bottom of his pocket. I polished his best dark brown shoes for him – chosen by my mother, who knew that you always wore brown shoes with grey – but somehow on him they lost their shine in five minutes. They all went off in Uncle Sidney's Rover, despite the protests of my father that that would mean Uncle Sidney having to come back to our house again. It would have been more sensible for my father to have followed Uncle Sidney in the Austin – petrol, for some reason, was the one thing he never minded fiddling a little extra of – but Uncle Sidney actually liked driving, even in the blackout. And of course he liked giving people a lift in the Rover, which was indeed a nice car, not fast, despite the makers calling it a Sportsman's Saloon, but beautifully made with an air of quiet opulence, solid without being ponderous, with really accurate steering and a clutchless gear-change if you wanted it; they don't make them like that any more.

However, my father and mother went off to the place in Manchester owned by a mate of my Uncle Sidney's and were rather noisy and giggly when they returned at midnight. I couldn't sleep; I lay awake in the darkness imagining an accident in the Rover, the Rover colliding with the La Salle coupé and the Graham-Paige sedanca de ville, putting the light on and reading last week's *Hotspur*, falling asleep and deliberately trying to dream my favourite dream of being the captain of a space-ship but only succeeding in dreaming of Heinkels and Junkers raining down bombs, then going into the sitting-room, the white flesh above the stocking-tops, the gleam of the nylon, the darker duller double-knit band at the top, awake again with the light on, looking at the wallpaper with its pattern of gnomes and rabbits and squirrels, red on a pink background, a wallpaper which I hated and which my father had promised to replace by something less babyish. Apart from the wallpaper, the furniture was adult: a three-quarter-size divan bed, a dark oak wardrobe and dressing-table, a bureau with a bedside lamp on it, a large old dark wooden chest in which I kept my toys, and a whitewood bookcase which was only a quarter full. The floor was covered with blood-red lino which smelt rather more strongly than lino usually does; the old term 'oilcloth' would have described it more accurately. There were two large pictures, one of Sopwith Camels and Fokker triplanes in a dogfight over the Western Front, another of Boy Cornwall beside his gun at the Battle of Jutland. I had chosen them originally, but by now I was sick of them; the war that was actually going on was far more interesting, though I was well aware that it would be over long before I had any chance to fight in it.

I heard Auntie Ada and my Uncle Sidney's voices, then the door slamming; he would be taking her home. I lost track of time, kept going backwards and forwards; the door opened downstairs, and I heard Uncle Sidney's voice, then, my hearing suddenly acute, the sound of a gas-ring plopping on, then I was back into a half-dream driving the La Salle coupé faster and faster, crashing into the Rover, into the Austin, then awake again and hearing steps coming up the stairs slowly and hesitatingly. The door was slightly ajar; a low-voltage bulb was always left alight on the landing; the door opened and my father stumbled in. I closed my eyes, and lay still, breathing evenly. He stood swaying over me, smelling of Burmese cheroots and whisky and, sharply and sourly, of wine. He bent down, nearly falling, and kissed my forehead. 'My little lad,' he said thickly, 'my little pride and joy.' He turned and stumbled out. I heard him go into the bathroom, then there was a thud. 'Fuck it!' he said. 'Fuck the – the – bloody – buggering – thing!' I hadn't heard the first word before, nor had I ever heard him speak like that before. Then he gulped very loudly. 'Oh Christ! Oh Jesus!' I heard the sound of vomiting.

Then there was my Uncle Sidney's voice, cool and amused and sober – 'Get it up, Len. Get it off your chest, man.' Once again there was the sound of vomiting, harsher this time, half coughing, half barking, not like a dog but like a sealion I'd heard once on the radio.

'He's not used to the hard stuff,' my mother said. 'Not like you, you devil. You *are* a rotten devil, a rotten scheming devil. Aren't you?'

I remember the words exactly, remember their tone exactly, because once again the tone – intimate, affectionate, half mocking, half admiring, didn't match the words. My father retched painfully, then coughed strongly, not like a sealion this time, and said in a thick, surprised voice: 'I'm very, very – very tired. Tired. Fuck it!' There was the sound of scrabbling feet and then a heavy thud and the almost explosive sound of the WC lid falling.

'Christ!' my uncle said, 'he's falling asleep on us. Give me a hand, Val.' I heard him panting. 'God, he's heavier than he looks.' His voice became cajoling. 'Come on, lad. Beddy bye-byes then. Sleep it off, there's a good boy . . .'

My eyes were closing despite myself; I heard footsteps, then a snore, then my mother's voice and my uncle's voice dropping away, whispering, whirling, dropping down, taking me into the driver's seat of the La Salle, dropping down faster and faster into the town, the car swaying on its springs down the winding road into the town, Jock Finnart smiling, weighing out the pear-drops again and again, the paper bag growing in size, larger than me now, and then awake and hearing my mother's voice whimpering, a little meandering childish whimper, steadily rhythmical like some nonsense song, then shouting, and then I was out of bed, half asleep, and went to the door but it was locked and I was shouting: 'Mother, Mother! What is it, Mother?'

A door opened, feet shuffled. How many feet shuffled? Half asleep still, I imagined four, six, eight, ten furry feet, clawed feet, mailed feet, killer's feet.

The door opened. I rushed towards my mother and hugged her; she put her arms round me, then moved away from me. Her face was flushed and she seemed to be trembling. 'Quiet now,' she said. 'Go to sleep.'

'You cried out, Mother, you did, you did. I heard you –'

'You were dreaming. Go back to sleep.' She led me back to my bed. She didn't put the light on. There was something odd about the way she moved, there was tension in it, but there was also a lack of constraint, a fluidity which was almost beautiful; she was moving like a sleepwalker.

'Where's Dad? Is he ill? Will he die?'

'Hush,' she said, tucking me in, still with the same sleepwalker's fluidity. 'Your father's asleep. He'll be all right in the morning.' She patted my head. 'Don't let me hear another sound from you now.' She closed the door behind her. And I was asleep almost as she closed it, and in the morning I took it for granted, so far had it been from my usual experience, that I had dreamed it all.

When I went downstairs my mother and Uncle Sidney were sitting in the kitchen drinking tea. There were the remains of bacon and eggs on my uncle's plate. He winked at me, his face rosy. 'Don't tell anyone about the bacon and eggs, Sonny,' he said. 'A little present – there's some for you too. But one word to anyone, just one word' – he pulled his face into a look of menace, his lips drawn snarling across his large white strong teeth – 'and Jimmy Knocker will get you and make you into dripping.'

'There isn't any Jimmy Knocker,' I said. I had been frightened of Jimmy Knocker once – I had visualised him as ten foot tall, skeletally thin, with a long black cloak, and a dead-white face with yellow fangs – but one night when we heard the bombers over Manchester I'd decided that he'd been killed by a bomb. Strangely enough, he resurrected himself after the War when I was nine; I still dream about him.

'Don't fill his head with daft ideas,' my mother said sharply. 'He has quite enough as it is.' She looked paler than usual, and there were dark circles under her eyes.

Uncle Sidney laughed. 'Len woke him up. Poor little Sonny. God, old Len was well away . . .' His jacket was off and hanging over the chair; his white shirt was the same one that he'd worn the day before, but it still gave the impression of being immaculate. His face was smoothly shaven with no cuts and no patches left unshaven; his sideboards, a little longer than was the fashion then, were ended neatly, instead of unevenly like my father's, and the back of his neck was smooth. He told me once that he had his hair trimmed every week to avoid looking alternately like a convict and a scruff. I didn't always like him, and particularly not that morning, but I always admired him and wanted to be like him when I grew up.

'What do you mean, well away, Uncle Sidney?' I asked.

'Well,' said my uncle, lighting two Passing Clouds and passing my mother one, 'let us say he'd had a few. Whisky and wine and brandy and then more whisky –'

'Don't talk like that about the boy's father,' my mother said sharply.

'Hell, I'm not saying anything wrong. Len's not used to it, that's all. Why, I spill more in one evening than he drinks in a year –'

'He's a good man,' my mother said. I noticed to my surprise that her eyes were moist.

My uncle rose, went over to her and put his hand on her shoulder. 'Of course he is, Val. One of the best –'

My mother shook off his hand. 'He's worth ten of you, Sidney.' She hissed out the words; my uncle shrugged and went back to his seat. In the kitchen with its yellow distempered walls and red tiles which never seemed clean despite ferocious scrubbing he seemed for a moment too large, too self-assured, too much the big businessman slumming it. There was a pile of dirty crockery in the sink and the gas oven needed cleaning and the red tablecloth over the small deal table was crumpled and stained; whatever faults my mother may have had she was a good housewife, and my uncle's presence seemed to accentuate the dirt and disorder.

'He *is* worth ten of me,' my uncle said reflectively. 'He's a decent hard-working chap and I'm a rotten sod. Always was.' He grinned disarmingly. 'That's why I've got on.'

'Mind you don't get on into jail,' my mother said. She was wearing a dark brown dress, lisle stockings, and a pinafore; she was a different woman from yesterday. She looked around the kitchen. 'God, this looks like Rammey's ranch . . .'

'Who's Rammey?' I asked.

'It's a saying.' She began to clear the table. 'Get yourself some milk, Jimmy. I can't bear looking at this kitchen any longer . . .'

'Can't I have some bacon and eggs?' I went to the larder – actually no more than a large cupboard built into the wall – and got out a bottle of milk.

'You can have bacon and eggs for your dinner.' She turned on the hot-water tap at the sink, her back to my uncle.

My father came into the kitchen rubbing his eyes. He was in his shirtsleeves and collarless; there was blood on his shirt and several cuts on his face. 'Where's the aspirin, Val?'

'In the sideboard, where they usually are.'

My father grunted and went into the sitting-room. He returned with the aspirin, sat down with his elbows on the table, poured himself a cup of tea with a shaking hand, and swallowed the aspirin. Then he lit a Woodbine and started coughing. 'God, I feel like death!'

'I can't think why you don't stay in bed,' my mother said, clattering crockery into the hot water. 'Do you think they can't run the business without you?'

'I'll be all right,' my father said. His eyes were bloodshot and the shadows under them were even darker than those under my mother's eyes. More than ever he looked an inferior version of my Uncle Sidney and, subtly, as if every bone in his body had been broken and badly reset; and there was still hanging around him an unmistakable odour of stale liquor.

'You're not going to work today,' my mother said. 'I'll phone the office and tell them you have a bilious attack, which is true enough.' She took hold of him by the shoulders. 'Get back upstairs and I'll bring you a hot-water bottle and some fresh tea.'

'This is all right,' my father said. 'I've got to go today; there's a pile of work waiting –'

'The tea isn't all right,' my mother said. 'It's like ink now, and it's stone-cold. What do you say it's all right for? You don't have to say it's all right when it isn't, you great mardy fool.' Her voice rose. 'That's your trouble. Every damned thing's all right. Everyone makes a fool out of you –'

My father put his hands to his head. 'Quiet, for Christ's sake, your voice is going right through my head.' He rose. 'I think I will go to bed.' He nodded at my uncle. 'See you, Sidney.'

'See you,' my uncle said.

My father went out of the kitchen, walking very slowly. I noticed that he had no socks on and that his shoelaces were unfastened. For some reason the sight of his white thin ankles and the trailing shoelaces made me sorry for him and angry with him at the same time.

My uncle sighed, looking suddenly older, rose abruptly, and put on his jacket.

'I'd better be off and earn an honest bob.' He grinned. 'Or rather a dishonest bob.'

My mother had returned to the sink. 'I shan't be seeing you for a while, shall I?' she said.

'I'll be back when Len's got over his hangover, make him think over what I proposed to him last night.'

'He won't,' she said, her back to him.

'For God's sake, Val, I'm serious. Now's the chance, before the competition starts –'

'He'll go his own way,' she said. Her voice was flat and without expression. 'He'd be no good in your kind of business, he's too trusting.' She turned to face him. There were soap-suds on her hands and the hot water had reddened them; as I look back I remember too the smell of the soap, harsh and abrasive but oily.

'He's a clever man,' my uncle said. 'And he's thorough. Slow but thorough.'

'He's too trusting,' my mother said. Her eyes moistened again. 'He's too damned trusting.'

'I'll try him again just the same,' my uncle said. 'When the booze has drained out.' He moved towards my mother as if to kiss her; she stared at him coldly. He gave her a little wave. 'See you, Val. See you, Sonny.' He ruffled my hair as he went out.

My mother stood staring after him and then, when the door had closed behind him, caught me up in her arms and hugged me. I could hear her heart beating. Then she kissed me fiercely, something she wasn't given to doing. Her hands felt very hot through my jersey and now tears were running down her cheeks.

That is all out now, the moment when the wound was inflicted. I don't think that I've missed anything out. I can't even now make a brief explicit statement about it; I am well aware of what happened that day and that night – or rather the small hours – and I am well aware now that it didn't happen for the first time. And all I can do is to remember all the circumstances – the uniform of the sniper, the make and calibre of his gun, the direction and strength of the wind, the time of day, the visibility – but I still cannot name the wound. It is painful enough to remember the circumstances; the temptation is to be content that the wound is no longer crippling, no longer stinking and purulent. But I have to go on to the day I returned to school.

I don't want to describe my schooldays; on the academic side at least I was taught to read and write and count very quickly. Most of us were: in those days it was taken for granted that that was why you went to school in the first place. No one bothered about whether we were happy or outgoing or well adjusted. I didn't enjoy school very much, but nobody cared whether I did or not. Most of my schoolmates were going to go into the mines and the mills anyway. I mixed quite well with them for the simple reason that if any of them hit me I hit them back. This is one reason why I'll always be grateful to my Uncle Sidney, perhaps the only reason. 'If anyone thumps you, Sonny, you thump them,' he said to me just before my first day at school. 'Never turn the other cheek. Never cry. Never expect anyone to look after you. Thump them back. And if they're bigger than you, kick 'em on the shins . . .' I've followed his advice all my life and it's worked out very well. I didn't get bullied at school, despite being different from the rest because of my father having a white-collar job and his own house and a car, and despite me being rather better dressed and having a bath every day and, though far from having a Standard English accent, not having as strong a Lancashire accent as the rest.

The school itself was a few minutes' walk from my home and had been built in 1935. It was in red brick because a relation of a prominent member of the Education Committee had a relative who had a lot of red bricks on his hands, and the red brick was now almost black. There was a Mixed Infants' and a Junior Girls' and a Junior Boys' section; at eleven everyone sat for the Eleven Plus and went either to Wardwick Boys' Grammar School, Wardwick Girls' Grammar School, or Felton High School in the town. Felton High School concentrated on metalwork and woodwork for the boys and domestic science for the girls; what help this was to them in the mines and the mills I've never been able to fathom.

Actually, the school could have been much worse. The playgrounds were of asphalt, but it was on the northern perimeter of the estate, so there were quite extensive playing-fields. And the coke-fired heating system was relatively modern and efficient and the classrooms large and airy. The staff, I realise now, were keen. There were only two men, the headmaster, Dick Snow, who was approaching retiring age, and the art master, Tim Millbeck, a small man in his middle fifties; they did their jobs reasonably well, I suppose, but they don't come into the story.

What comes into the story now is Miss Scott, my teacher in Class Two. She was, I suppose, about twenty-four. She was very slim with grey-blue eyes and ash-blonde hair which she wore in a bun. I used to wonder how it stayed in place. She was, as I say, very slim, but she was fond of linen shirt blouses and sometimes when she bent over my desk I would catch a glimpse of the division between her breasts, which were small but indisputably there; the division was a shadow rather than a cleft, but a glimpse of it would colour the whole day with happiness, a happiness almost as fierce as my secret pleasure, but with no tinge of guilt. And she had marvellous legs, though she was careful with her skirts. She was a good teacher too, kind and gentle and patient; she left after a year, to get married, and nothing was the same for me again.

I remember her best reading to us from *Winnie-the-Pooh*, the ash-blonde hair glowing against the buff-distempered walls, the eyes of the children open as the beaks of fledglings are open, each almost ferociously still, each transported out of the wretched little town and the view of scrubby wasteland and pitheads and chimneys and black smoke and grey skies, and her smell, her wonderful smell of soap and face powder and healthy woman dominating the smell of chalk and ink and the wet acrid smell of the radiators and the smell of children who only had a bath and a change of underwear once a week, if indeed as often as that. I remember that, and I remember her fiancé, a RAF sergeant-pilot, coming to take her home on his BSA 500. He was a big man with a red face and a Pilot Kite moustache – a huge, bushy moustache then fashionable, partly, I suspect, because it was over regulation length. I hated him out of pure jealousy; he made me aware that she wasn't for me, would never be for me. If I hadn't seen him with her I could have believed that she only existed when I saw her, that she was put in a cupboard in the classroom when I went home, emerging from it only a moment before I came to school the next day. I didn't even want her to have a home away from the school, I wanted her to exist only for me.

I remember too the day when she'd been shopping at lunchtime. She'd come into the classroom breathless and put down a paper bag on the desk. That day she was reading from *The Wind in the Willows*. We'd reached the part where Mole is having a picnic with Ratty. I was entranced like the rest, particularly with the list of foods, some of which were to me totally exotic, when I caught sight of something protruding from the paper bag. What I saw was blue rayon with a scalloped edging; moving my position slightly, I could see, the bag not being properly closed, that what was inside it was a pair of French knickers. That was the term used then to denote short knickers without elastic on the legs; even at my age then the term had connotations of sexuality if not of downright immorality.

The sight of them excited me almost unbearably. It wasn't the French knickers in themselves, it was the fact that they were Miss Scott's, that Miss Scott at some time somewhere – and it couldn't be in any ordinary room in any ordinary house; it would be inside walls of rose-coloured crystal; there would be a fountain and music inside and fireworks outside – would put them on, it meant the great wonderful secret revealed then concealed, yet not concealed but decorated, accentuated; and I felt without touching myself, without willing it, the unmistakable beginning between my legs of that secret pleasure which always before had depended upon my hand. And this honestly wasn't lust. I was well aware that I had to keep quiet about it; I felt that it would shock Miss Scott if she knew, but that was only because neither she nor anyone else would understand. Perhaps nobody would understand even now; perhaps all that they'd see would be a dirty little boy, certainly a precocious little boy, even a perverted little boy. That wasn't it at all. I was worshipping, I was loving, I would have done anything in the world for her – except that I couldn't think of anything; I had nothing to give her. The giving was all on her side without her knowing it; looking at her and looking at the French knickers I was steered gently but firmly in the proper sexual direction. I suppose that today we'd have had a dialogue, we'd have talked it through; but those days dialogues about sex, between teacher and pupil, were literally, and I mean literally, unthinkable. And this is just as well, because for an adult even to have talked to me about the happenings of the day before would have been completely disastrous. *Winnie-the-Pooh* — I imagined clean white houses, trees, flowers, grass, clear sparkling rivers — and Miss Scott's gentle wholesome voluptuousness was exactly what I needed, a reassurance of the goodness and holiness of the female, the never-cloying sweetness of that rapturously different flesh. I'm sure now that she was a virgin; there were a lot about those days, even though there was a war on and men had the *be kind to me I may never come back* trump card to play. Maybe I speak only from hindsight, but it seems to me that she was too tranquil to have been anything else but a virgin.

In an ideal world Miss Scott would have perceived that I was unhappy about something, and a delicate and tender relationship would have sprung up between us. This isn't an ideal world — if it were there'd be no one in it like my Uncle Sidney — and Miss Scott regarded me no differently from the rest, except no doubt that I smelled rather cleaner. And this quite satisfied me; I didn't, so to speak, expect the Holy Virgin to come down from her pedestal and wipe the sweat from my brow.

That was the day when I first made friends with Jeff Hunstanton. He was large for his age, about two inches taller than me and much broader, with red hair and green eyes, and the term before he had fought with me almost every day. He didn't really want to bully me; he wanted me to acknowledge him the better fighter, and I never would. He lived in the next street to me and his father, a large red-haired man, was what was then called a commercial traveller in soaps and various toilet wares; he had served in the First World War and had been gassed badly enough to prevent him from serving in the Second. He was widowed at thirty and married again late in life — or late in life according to working-class standards — and

Jeff was his son by his second marriage. He was a Socialist and my father a Conservative, which was one of the things which Jeff and I fought about; not that either of us really cared at the time.

At break that afternoon Jeff sidled over to me and said in a low voice: 'I think Miss Scott is nice.'

I didn't quite know how to take it; I even rather resented him admiring her too. 'She's all right,' I said.

'You were looking at her with your mouth wide open. Like a fish.'

'I was listening to the story.'

'You don't listen with your mouth.'

'I listen just how I like,' I snapped.

'Aw, come on. You know you like her.'

'Everybody does. Absolutely everybody.'

'Ma Brown doesn't. She's too pretty, Ma Brown says. Thinks too much of herself.'

'Phooey to Ma Brown!'

He whispered into my ear. 'Do you know how babies are made?'

''Course I know.' For no reason my heart was suddenly beating fast.

'The man gets out his John Thomas –' he giggled '– and he sticks it into the woman's hole. Did you know that?' He was grinning. There was rain on the wind; I looked away from him over the low brick wall and saw an Army convoy on the road outside the school. I found myself suddenly ashamed, ashamed of my own body, ashamed even for a second of having looked at Miss Scott and her French knickers.

'I don't believe it. How can it stick in?'

'It sort of gets big and stiff.'

On the left was a low wall and the playing-fields and beyond them a patch of wasteland; the Army convoy passed by and I reflected that I'd never be in the Army, never fire a gun, never pilot an aeroplane, never drive a torpedo boat; everything would pass by, everyone was going far away into adventure and faraway places, and I would stay here.

'It's not true,' I said fiercely. 'You're a rotten liar –' I stopped; the sense of shame took over again. 'You're making it up. You've got a mucky mind.' But I spoke with no real conviction; various scraps of overheard adult conversation, a memory of dogs coupling, and worst of all, what I had seen and heard the day before, joined together to corroborate the information.

'My Dad told me.' He spoke with a certain pride. 'He says I might as well get it right. People who don't get it right are in trouble later on.'

'What trouble?' It occurred to me that now that I knew, I was in trouble; because now what I felt for Miss Scott had somehow been spoiled; I was in trouble because I didn't know what was happening to me, except that I didn't like it.

'They have babies without being married. And worse things.'

'What worse things?'

'He wouldn't tell me.' He looked at me curiously. 'You've gone white.'

'I haven't.' I punched him playfully in the belly. 'Race you to the gates.'

We became friends after that and, whatever has happened since, I've always been grateful for it. I expect to some extent our friendship was founded upon the fact that our fathers were roughly at the same level, except that my father had bought his own car and his father's Hillman Minx had been provided by the firm; but we were both better off than the rest and, as I've indicated, had a bath every day. Not that during the War anybody was poor; there was plenty of overtime for everyone and the women all worked, as they always had done. But there was still a difference between us and the rest, and it made sense for us to stick together. And Jeff, despite fighting with me for the whole term, had an amiable easygoing nature. I am always stirred up about something, always fiercely wanting something, and will not be quiet until I'm in my grave. I'm up and down, I change as the wind changes, but Jeff was always the same.

And this is all that matters of my days at the primary school. I added to that first basic information, for the most part getting the facts right, but now and again being dragged screaming into the world of myth. There was the story of the boy who stuck it in his little sister but who peed instead of coming, and killed her. And the classic story of the couple, married but not to each other, who got inextricably joined together and had to be taken to hospital under a blanket, and who were finally released by the man's penis being amputated. And of course, out of the mists of the past, there was the story of Fatty Arbuckle whose penis was so big that it killed a girl. Certainly Jeff didn't always paint a rosy picture of sex. I got over all this, though; what it took me a long time to get over, if indeed I have ever properly got over it, was what happened the following Monday.

I came down the stairs just as my father was opening a letter. It was in a plain white envelope and his name and address were typewritten. It was a misty morning and the flap of the letter-box was open, letting in cold air. From the kitchen I could smell black pudding frying. My father looked at the letter; his eyes widened. Then his mouth

66

opened as if to scream. I didn't see that expression on a human face again until I saw a reproduction of Francis Bacon's Screaming Man. He was all the time looking straight through me. It was almost in my mind that the black pudding could be human flesh, a cut of rump, a slice off the belly – and then he saw me and did not scream but crammed the letter into his pocket and picked up the other letter from the floor.

That is the easiest part, because I was there; I saw it. It still hurts, but I saw how he was hurt. The staring eyes, the mouth almost square, the silent scream – distressing though it was, I saw it. There is no mystery. There is no mystery about his feelings after he left the house for work. He said nothing about the letter to my mother, and spoke very little at breakfast, but in any event he didn't talk much at breakfast. He didn't talk much at any time. It would have been better if he had; but there wasn't much that a boy of seven could do about it, particularly since he never understood what was wrong until it was too late.

What I next have to face is the memory of the Flying Horse at Pidswell on the road to Parbold. Nothing need be said about Parbold except that it's a village north of Wigan which no one will ever visit unless they have urgent business there. Nothing need be said about Pidswell either; there are four small dairy farms in the vicinity, a sub-post office and general stores, and of course the Flying Horse. I don't suppose that there's much else to do in Pidswell except to drink in the Flying Horse, a square Accrington-brick building dating from the 1890s, with a taproom, a saloon bar, a bar parlour for men only, and a snug. The walls are whitewashed and the seats plain wood except in the saloon bar and the bar parlour. There the chairs and benches are padded.

The road to Pidswell is narrow and winding and begins north of the estate; you can see where it begins from the school gates. It's about three miles' walk, a reasonable distance to walk to build up a thirst, and sufficient to get rid of some of the more toxic effects of slaking that thirst. This was my father's local; he never went in the car but preferred to walk. I think that he enjoyed the walk – though the scenery was not, to say the least of it, a feast for the eye – and I think that, unlike most motorists in those days, he didn't like to drink and to drive.

He didn't say much that Monday evening when he came home, and I had already forgotten the incident of the letter. My mother was rather surprised when he said that he was going to the Flying Horse, because he generally only went there on a Friday evening. His quietness was nothing out of the ordinary; but I did notice that he wasn't really either reading his book – it was, I remember, a Tiger Standish thriller by Sidney Horler – or listening to the radio. My mother raised her eyebrows when he said he was going to the Flying Horse, but made no comment. That's something significant to remember; in that place at that period most people were miserly with both greetings and farewells. One would have imagined that hello and goodbye and good evening and good morning and how are you and the rest were forbidden as being too luxurious, that everybody was bound by a verbal sumptuary law.

At midnight my father still had not returned and my mother phoned the police. I knew this because I awoke at a quarter to midnight and knew instantly that something was wrong. The door was slightly ajar and I could sense that my mother and father were not in their room. And I heard my Auntie Ada's voice downstairs; I knew that she wouldn't be there unless something were wrong. I lay awake for a moment staring at Boy Cornwall beside his gun; it was near the door and I could make out the outline of the gun. For the first time it occurred to me that guns were actually made in order to kill people, and I looked away from the picture. I thought of my father on the Saturday before, when he'd taken me to Finnart's to spend my Saturday threepence. I generally went by myself, but my father said that he wanted to stretch his legs. It was a cold afternoon with a steel-grey sky; the roses which bloom here in the South until the beginning of November were already beginning to wither. There were no colours but black and grey; there was no frost as yet but you could smell it in the air.

Finnart was drinking tea with whisky in it when we entered the shop. I realise now that I never once entered the shop when he wasn't drinking tea. But I remember that on that day the tea smelled of whisky.

'Hello, Len,' he said. 'You're looking a bit pale. Well, what would the war effort be without the British workingman?'

My father grunted something. It might have been a greeting, but it's more likely that it was instead of knocking Finnart down. Finnart had just told him that he didn't look well, which never cheers anyone up, and had also reminded my father that he wasn't in uniform, and, worst of all, had categorised him as working-class. My father could hardly have been more insulted. Perhaps his trouble was that he neither knocked Finnart down nor had answers ready which would have got under Finnart's skin.

My father lit a Woodbine and looked around the shop in the strange, lost way which was habitual to him. Even at my age it annoyed me; he looked so damned *humble*.

'More again,' Finnart said to me. 'Aren't you the wee lucky one?'

My father looked at him inquiringly.

'Only the other day he was here with money to burn.' The *r* in *burn* rolled like a kettledrum.

'You're not complaining are you, Jock?' my father asked.

'Och, no. Bring in the siller and I'll help you spend it.'

My father grunted again. 'What do they call those toy cars you were after? Those Yank toys?'

'Tootsie Toys,' I said, rather surprised. It wasn't that my father was mean or not interested in me; it was simply that he was unaware of anything beyond the fact that I liked toys in general.

'I don't see why you shouldn't have them whilst they're still here,' my father said, surprising me still more.

'Jim's already bought them,' Finnart said. 'His Uncle Sidney gave him the money.' The small grey eyes had narrowed. He took a mouthful of tea and whisky with relish.

My father looked at him coldly. 'Of course, I'd forgotten.' His voice was cold. He turned to me and said in the same tone. 'Buy yourself something else.' He put his hand in his pocket. 'How much did the Tootsie Toys cost?'

'A shilling,' I said. I couldn't quite fathom the reason for his coldness.

'Here's two shillings. Spend it.' He scrabbled in his pocket and brought out some ration coupons. 'Half a pound of Cadbury Dairy cubes,' he said. 'And half a pound of pear-drops.'

He flicked his ash on the gleaming red and white linoleum tiles; there was a flicker of annoyance on Finnart's face.

I bought a Dinky Toy lorry, a Carter Paterson van, and three comics. One was *Film Fun*, another *Tiger Tim's Weekly*, but I've forgotten the other one. What I haven't forgotten is the look of triumph on Finnart's face as we left the shop. But let me define it more closely: it was the anticipation of triumph.

I don't think that my father saw it; I do know that when we were outside the shop he used a word I hadn't heard him use before. 'The cunt,' he said, 'the nasty little Scottish *cunt*!' He looked at me sternly. 'Shouldn't have used that word. You're never to use it. Promise?'

'I promise,' I said, and took his arm; he walked more slowly than usual, his expression disturbed. I sometimes wish he'd been different, that he'd been quicker to react, not so slow and patient and trusting, not so damned *forbearing*. I wish even that he'd been angry with me about keeping my purchase of the Tootsie Toys secret. But he didn't talk about it again, and I didn't raise the matter.

I remembered all this when I awoke at a quarter to twelve and I found it hurting me, transfixing me with an almost unbearable sense of guilt. I endured it for a little while, then ran downstairs, into the living-room. 'Where's Dad?'

My mother and Auntie Ada looked at me in silence.

'Go back to bed,' my mother said. The patches of rouge were standing out on her cheeks.

'Where's Dad? *Where's Dad?*'

My Auntie Ada put her arm round me. Her body felt very stiff. I knew that she wore corsets; I had seen them once on the horsehair sofa at her cottage. They explained her invariably erect posture and her preference for hard upright chairs; they were stiffened with whalebone and no doubt could have stood up by themselves. Her face seemed stiff too, stiffened by the certainties – this was over thirty years ago – of Nonconformism. But just now it was open and crumpled and vulnerable.

'He'll be having supper with a friend, love,' she said.

'Won't have thought of phoning. We'll have something to say to him when he gets home, won't we, Val?'

My mother nodded, and lit a cigarette. She rarely smoked, but kept a packet of Du Maurier in a drawer in the bureau in the living-room. Du Maurier – in a red packet with a picture of the actor – were almost the only filter-tips on the market then; it's curious how these details stay in the mind.

My Aunt Ada kissed me, something which she normally only did for saying hello and goodbye. 'Go to bed, love,' she said. 'Don't worry.'

But almost as soon as I closed the door I heard her say 'Oh God, it's not like him to be so late –' and I ran up the stairs and went to bed holding the Carter Paterson van for comfort, why I didn't know, burying my head under the bedclothes, trying to pretend that I was dreaming it all.

When I came down in the morning I looked through the living-room window to see my mother getting into a police car. It was a black Wolseley, solid and old-fashioned even then. They had an illuminated badge in the centre of the grille; the lights were on and the badge was a small yellow patch of light. There seemed to be almost as much illumination from the badge as from the masked headlights. It was drizzling hard and the dawn was dribbling a pale washed-out pink over the grey sky. The criss-cross of black tape on the window for a moment gave the room the air of a prison cell. The living-room was untidier than usual, with a tea-tray on the small oak dining-table with two half-full cups on it, newspapers and knitting patterns and a half-knitted sweater on the sofa, and an overflowing ashtray on the small coffee-table by my mother's armchair on the left-hand side of the fireplace. There was more than the usual amount of litter on the mantelpiece — letters, postcards, official forms, insurance books, reels of cotton, packets of needles — and the large gilt clock with the shepherds and shepherdesses on its face, a wedding present which never varied by more than a minute a week, had stopped at midnight. I knew that it had stopped before I looked at it, because I missed its steady ticking as soon as I entered the room.

'Where's Dad?' I asked.

Auntie Ada looked at me dumbly and burst into tears.

'You'll have to know,' she said, half to herself. 'You'll have to know.'

I was shocked at her weeping; it was something which I'd never seen before. She moved to the sofa and sat down heavily, taking out a handkerchief from her large black leather handbag. The handkerchief smelled of camphor. She wiped her eyes and put back the handkerchief. She took my hand.

'Your father's dead.'

I think that she was absolutely right to give it to me straight and unadorned, not to try to put it off, not to raise any false hopes, not even to tell me that I must be very brave. The pain and the loss rushed at me savagely, the sword slashed, the gun fired, the forceps wrenched out the tooth, the worst came all at once, and the worst was over. Aunt Ada rocked me in her arms, crying again, her corsets creaking slightly, the smell of camphor growing stronger, as if she were weeping camphor; I've hated the smell of the stuff ever since.

I could not cry then but I cried later. I don't remember when and how I learned about the circumstances of my father's death, except that I have always had a picture in my mind of the road to Pidswell — no more than a narrow bumpy track through wasteland at first, then winding between flat turnip fields for about a mile, then forking to the left. The left fork is a dead end; you bear right for Pidswell and the Flying Horse. There are turnip fields beside the fork to the left; they end in wasteland and swamp, and at the centre of the swamp is a small stagnant pond with steep sloping sides. It isn't more than five feet deep – a big puddle rather than a pond – but it is deep enough to kill a drunken man with a weak heart. My father had drunk much more than he usually did that night, he hadn't talked to anyone, and he'd left a quarter of an hour before closing time. He had his torch and knew the road well, but it was a dark night and he'd had five pints of bitter and four large whiskies.

All this was kept out of the newspapers. My father, though not a gregarious man, was respected in the town, and my Auntie Ada was not without influence. I think too that his cronies at the Flying Horse felt that they should have insisted upon seeing him safely home, despite his protestations that he didn't need anybody and despite his obvious desire to be alone.

I understand that now. I understand his desire that night to be out of the house, to be alone for a while, then to find oblivion in company, surrounded by people yet not involved with them. I'm sure that he didn't tell anyone what was on his mind; perhaps it would have been better for him if he had. I haven't thought about his death for many years, though now I have come to understand him more and more. And to love him more and more, now that it is too late. Sometimes it breaks my heart that he can't see me now; the fruit of his loins up there with Uncle Sidney but well on the right side of the law. And he would have liked his grandchildren. I would have had him here to stay and I'd have given him all the thrillers he wanted – brand-new ones, never touched by anyone before – and

I'd have bought him new clothes – comfortable and amply cut, of the best materials – and I'd have given him Löwenbräu beer and barley wine and single malt whisky and Harrods real pork sausages and a new car if he'd wanted one, something decent, a bit out of the ordinary run, an Alfetta or an Audi 80 with a stereo radio and cassette player. He liked to go to the pictures, and I'd have taken him to cinemas in the West End to see them new, before anyone in Lancashire, and on first-rate equipment in mint condition.

Though indeed I don't know whether he'd have wanted all those things, except perhaps the grandchildren. I've had to reconstruct his character from what others told me and from a few old photos; there are naturally no written records. I am not sure now how much of what I know is from my own memory; since no one remembers much of what happens before the age of five there were only a couple of years when he registered for me as an individual human being. My impression is that he never wanted very much, that he was all for his comforts and a quiet life, that he didn't entirely like the town he lived in or the way he earned his living, but he made the best of it. I don't think that he wanted to change anything, but that he hoped to God things wouldn't get any worse.

That isn't me, nor, with all his faults, was it my Uncle Sidney. I only wish that he'd been more like my Uncle Sidney, that he'd *wanted* things. I only wish he'd been less trusting from the start. What was in the letter that hurt him so much? That evening I caught my mother throwing it into the fire; it had been in his pocket when the police found him face down in the pond. She never talked about it. I don't want to ask her. Not because I care about hurting her, but because it would hurt me too much. I have a pretty fair notion of what was in it, because I am now aware of just what kind of triumph Jock Finnart was anticipating. At the time I didn't connect him with the letter, nor did I perceive the importance of the letter. The *idea* of an anonymous letter hurting someone intolerably was one I couldn't grasp; it was my *instincts* that told me that the letter had hurt my father. You don't need a degree in medicine to know that it's agony when someone's kicked in the balls. You don't even need to know that the balls are especially sensitive; cause and effect are plain to see.

It would be pleasant to record that Jock Finnart was unmasked and duly punished; but nothing happened. If he wrote other anonymous letters I never heard of it; but then no one ever heard of ours. And what evidence have I except my instincts? When I went to the shop afterwards I felt a faint queasiness; but Jock merely put on an appropriate expression, said that he was grieved to hear of my tragic loss, and sighed heavily. He did not, however, refer to my Uncle Sidney again.

And now the darkness comes, darkness falling over the ranch-style houses, the Georgian-style houses, the 1930 cubist-style houses, the no-particular-style houses, falling over the sleek lawns, the roses and the torch lilies and the hydrangea and the silver birches and the sycamores and the double garages and the swimming-pools; the lights are going on in the houses all up and down Sugar Hill, and I put on the wall-lights by the sofa, go into the hall to switch on the low-wattage night-light bulb on the landing, walk slowly up the broad staircase – very trendy once with a rope for the bannister-rail, which I've had boxed in with plain white wood – and into the children's rooms. Sharon first, across the bed like a starfish, clutching a rag doll. I put the duvet over her again and kiss her moist

76

forehead. Gareth next, as dark as Sharon is fair, his arms by his sides, scowling a little even in sleep. I touch his forehead gently; it is perfectly dry. The duvet is neatly over him, his teddy-bear has its arms by its sides too. The walls of each room have a large peg-board on one side and are painted in washable sky-blue for Gareth, pink for Sharon; Sharon's room is very tidy, Gareth's, despite his disciplined posture, always a mess. They are both happy children: the pressure isn't upon them yet. They haven't known any places which weren't pleasant places, breathed any air which wasn't smoke-free, met anyone who – outwardly at least – wasn't civilised and agreeable. They will go to private schools with children like themselves, and Gareth will get a job like mine, and Sharon will marry a man with a job like mine. They will live in the Home Counties too, because that's where the jobs like mine are and where the jobs will continue to be.

Gareth has a nightlight bulb over his bed; despite his aggressiveness he's inclined to be nervous. But Sharon won't have one. She's never been afraid of the dark. I tell them that I love them equally, but that's a lie. It's Sharon I love the most, because she loves me most, because she demonstrates it, because she's Daddy's girl. Why is Daddy's girl a term which is used with an amused indulgence and Mummy's boy a term which is purely one of contempt? Not that Gareth is Mummy's boy; he is alternately withdrawn and aggressive, sparing with his displays of affection.

I go down the stairs again and into the kitchen and take my fourth can of lager from the refrigerator. The dark has come; already it has settled down over Lancashire – earlier sunsets, later springs, earlier winters, snow on high ground even in September – and my mother will have closed her hairdresser's shop and will be having a

77

quiet drink in some cocktail bar. There will be a man around somewhere; there always is a man around somewhere for my mother, even in her sixties. She has kept her figure with the aid of dieting and made-to-measure corsets, and her face has been lifted more than once. The hair is still black, the face a smooth perfect mask; only around the neck does the flesh show her age, sagging like a turkey's. But the old men whom she has a facility of picking up don't care about this; and the younger men in whom she occasionally indulges only see her, I suppose, as so much money on the hoof.

I met one of them once some four years ago when I was visiting a shirt manufacturer in Lancashire. I never did catch his surname; he was introduced to me as Rolf, which I'm sure wasn't his baptismal name.

Rolf had called in unexpectedly just before I arrived, my idea being to take my mother out to dinner at my hotel and put her on a taxi back. But when I reached her house there was already this white Chev Impala convertible there taking up three-quarters of the road. I have moods in which I wouldn't mind something like that — flashy, high-powered, rather endearing in its brashness, expressly designed to make the Joneses green with envy — but I can't see Droylsden's shareholders wearing it. It was a bright June evening and the estate looked smarter than ever it had done in my childhood, each tiny front garden a blaze of flowers and each exterior glossy with paint. I saw that, where there had been a garden path before, there was a narrow drive and a new Marley garage.

I rang the bell — she'd had musical chimes installed — and she came to the door looking indefinably dishevelled. Her black hair was piled high and lacquered, with not a strand out of place; she had black fully-fashioned stockings with straight seams, the glass buttons on her red nylon

78

dress were all fastened, but she was still dishevelled. Was it the expression in her eyes – not sated quite, but having enjoyed the hors-d'œuvres? Or an especial smoothness about the face, the rich gloss which could only have one origin? That was soon after her first face-lift and the skin around her neck was still taut – a shade too taut, but not yet sagging – and her bosom was still two breasts rather than a unified protuberance; the cleft revealed by the V of the dress was a natural division rather than a sort of deep wrinkle.

Over the years since my father's death she'd gradually got rid of the old decorations and the old furniture; she used the sitting-room as a living-room now and called it the lounge; the living-room was a dining-room with oak panels and an oak G-plan dining-suite from Heals. The lounge was papered in pale grey and gold and there was a three-piece suite in gold satin which must have set her back, even then, a cool five hundred; there was a chandelier overhead and pink wall-lights and a walnut cocktail cabinet and a twenty-six-inch colour TV and a Telefunken radiogram and a nest of glass-topped walnut tables and thick grey fitted carpet and a standard lamp with a pink shade. She had gas-fired central heating now, of course, with gold-painted radiators and there was a white New World gas-fire. I probably have missed something out; I have a recollection of a walnut glass-fronted bookcase and a china-cabinet and a long coffee-table with a white and red mosaic top of the kind we were then selling at Droylsden's for a hundred and twenty. Considering that the suite was twice the dimensions of the old one and the sofa was a three-seater, I was surprised that she'd got everything in. The room smothered me, particularly since she had the gas-fire on; its only merit was that it smelled of prosperity, which may well be vulgar and materialistic but which is a great deal more agreeable than the smell of poverty and worry.

My mother kissed me on the cheek; she stood some five foot five inches in her high heels and felt strangely light in my grasp. Her breath smelt faintly of gin and tobacco; very faintly, for she'd taken a mouthwash or some mouth deodorant tablets. I remembered that when I was younger she would, if nothing else was available, rinse her mouth with eau-de-cologne: she had an obsession about bad breath, one of her few virtues. 'You're looking very well,' she said, and kissed me again, on the mouth. 'What a *lovely* suit.'

I was wearing a lightweight light grey mohair and a plain blue silk shirt with button-down collar and a blue and red silk Dior tie and dark brown wet-look Bally shoes, all from our own stock at Droylsden's.

'We've an unexpected visitor,' she said, preceding me into the lounge, where a young man was sitting smoking a large cigar.

She turned her face away from me as she gestured towards him, and lowered her voice. So I only caught 'This is Rolf' – and when she gave my name, I half waved my hand and said 'Hi'.

'Hi,' Rolf said. 'Heard a lot about you, man.'

'That's nice,' I said. 'That your car outside?'

'It could be yours,' he said. He held out a bunch of keys. His nails were rosy with a recent manicure, which was one good mark, plus another for his dark grey denim suit, plus one for dark brown suede chukka-boots, minus a half for a shirt and scarf which were pink and the wrong shade of pink. He was tall and thin, narrow-shouldered and not much more than thirty-seven in the chest, small-boned and frail-looking like most of his generation. His trousers were drawn tight at the crotch, and cut tight in any case; my mother couldn't resist a quick downwards glance, and I then realised his attraction for her, if I'd not realised it before.

I didn't take the car keys. 'Not for me,' I said. 'I've got to have a car anyone can service.'

'Hell,' he said, 'the Chev only needs it every ten thousand miles. In the States they build cars to go, with no sweat about maintenance. It's a great big underworked engine; it never does more than three thousand revs . . .'

In my Uncle Sidney's day if you wanted to get ahead you spoke something approximating Standard English, in my generation you spoke a sort of King's Road parody Standard English (though I didn't); but Rolf spoke a modified Liverpudlian that now, for obvious reasons, is socially OK.

'Have a little drinkie,' my mother said. She put her hand caressingly on Rolf's shoulder. 'No use trying to sell anything to Jim, love. He makes his living selling.'

'You know what I want,' Rolf said.

'It's so *dull*,' my mother said. 'Have some rum in it.'

Rolf shook his head. 'If I lose my licence I'm dead, honey.'

She pouted and left the room. Rolf watched her walk out, her hips swaying with a sort of prim abandon, and I was surprised to see physical desire on his face. Seeing it I felt an actual spasm of pain in the pit of my stomach. I lit a cigarette and sat down, keeping my eyes away from him.

My mother returned with a can of Coca-Cola; he opened it and moved to the cocktail cabinet and poured it into a tall glass, tilting the glass carefully so that it didn't foam over the rim.

'Drinkie for Sonny?' my mother asked me.

'Scotch,' I said. 'On the rocks.' I sipped it very slowly; it had the required effect of dulling the pain in my stomach.

'Rolf and I have a little business deal,' my mother said, pouring herself a small gin, inserting ice from the ice-bowl, and topping it up with tonic. She sat down beside Rolf; her skirt rode up over still-rounded knees and even the whisky couldn't dull the pain now. I tried to disregard it.

'What's your line, then?' I asked Rolf.

'This and that, this and that,' he said evasively. 'Buying and selling, man, buying and selling . . .'

My mother touched his knee lightly; her hands had not had the benefit of plastic surgery, for they were on the verge of being clawlike, with long red finger-nails.

'We sell a lot of things apart from hair-dos,' she said. 'The big suppliers are murder. All those forms . . . As bad as dealing with the damned Government. You know how it is, Sonny.'

Indeed Sonny knew how it was: if you have cash coming in, actual coin of the realm, you can always get some of it just for yourself and you don't record it, and then you buy supplies with coin of the realm and you don't record it because people like Rolf don't want their income recorded. And that is why so many small businesses declare such small incomes. Sonny understood and Sonny sympathised; but now the sweat had begun to stand out on his forehead and he was feeling actually physically sick and he excused himself and went to the rose-pink bathroom with the pink cover on the toilet seat and the mirror all round the walls and the pink phone by the toilet and the cabinet crammed with old medicines and half-used bottles of cologne and a ladies' Ronson shaver and a Remington men's shaver and four bottles of men's cologne – Canoe, Eau Sauvage, Imperial Leather, Brut – and tried to be sick but couldn't, and then gargled with mouthwash and sat on the toilet seat for a moment, his head in his hands.

I have to look at it like that because both the stomach pain and the mounting anger were as if happening to somebody else. That's something which one often reads about but which I at least hadn't experienced until then. The worst of it was that the person who felt both sick and angry wasn't really within my control. He was quite capable of running downstairs, running into the kitchen, grabbing a carving knife, and, hiding it behind his back, walking into the sitting-room and killing both Rolf and my mother. I wouldn't have been able to stop him. And it was not I but he who walked down the stairs. He didn't run, and I can see now why he didn't run; it would have alerted my mother and Rolf, since it would have been an odd thing to do, the steps being narrow and steep. He didn't go into the kitchen, but hesitated at the door, and went through the lounge, and into the smell of cigar-smoke and the smell, musky but floral, of my mother's Diorissimo, and sharp but faint, clear but blurred, only discernible if one was alert for it, the marine smell, more like seafood than fish, of sexual excitement: *he's been touching the old whore up.*

Just a quick touching up, up the nylon, up the double-knit at the top of the stocking, up the hot bare soft flesh, up inside the knickers, brushing smoothness of nylon again, up into the yielding yet muscular softness, the hairy softness, the wet sucking softness, the terrible dark softness, the spreading, *spreading*, dark softness, the utter *darkness*.

And to his horror Sonny had an erection and the anger grew as the darkness grew, as the erection grew, and he put his hand over his mouth and turned away, forming a plan to push away the darkness once and for all.

'Aren't you well, Sonny?' his mother asked him.

That was it, that was the trigger. 'Don't call me Sonny,' he said, trying to keep his tone light. 'I'm a big boy now.'

'Sorry, Jim,' his mother said. 'But honestly, you look *gruesome*. Can't I get you something?'

'I'll be all right,' I said, the erection subsiding and the stomach pain and the anger subsiding with it, fully in control again, the other person, the stranger, locked safely away deep down in my mind. 'I'll finish this drink and we'll be off.' The sweat was dying on my forehead now, the whisky was warming my stomach, the tension was over. It had, after all, been a pretty tough day for me, since there were various problems concerning the shirts, the main one being that we wanted a lot of what he had only a little of and a little of what he'd got a lot of. And he had a smart young graduate in the sales department hovering around, which almost convinced him that it was his function to sell the customer what he wanted the customer to buy and to hell with what the customer wanted. The smart young graduate had not of course realised that Droylsden's could do without the shirt manufacturer before the shirt manufacturer could do without Droylsden's. If I had gone away in a huff, Droylsden's would have lost, in terms of my salary and expenses, only about a hundred; the shirt manufacturer would have lost at least a thousand. As soon as I started to think about this, it confirmed the fact that I was in control. But it was a bad moment.

It's something else which I've held back until now. Why do I bring it out? Because I can't go on if I don't, because there's too much locked safely away deep down in my mind, because the adjective *safely* is no longer fully valid, because the prison has become overcrowded, because the prisoners are violent, because I'm sure that they have a plan. Messages tapped in code from cell to cell, files and knives and crowbars and guns smuggled in, flare-ups between prisoner and prisoner, between guard and guard. And then there are periods when it's all too quiet, when nobody breaks the rules, when it seems that they've all accepted the world of concrete and steel and double locks and bars as home, that they no longer hanker to flood the world outside, the rich world, the defenceless world, the world which they long to despoil and shatter.

I don't know why it must be now that it all comes out, that I look at myself, that I cease to live wholly in the present; but I know what happened to my father. Certainly he didn't commit suicide; he had, my Aunt Ada told me long afterwards, tried to scrabble up the bank, and it seems likely that his heart gave out during the attempt. In any case it was an unlikely method of committing suicide; the pond was scarcely deep enough to drown in at its deepest point. And he could swim: a swimmer can only drown by swimming deliberately too far. He brooded about the letter all day, probably read and re-read it, then went out to get thoroughly drunk. If he hadn't taken the wrong turning he'd probably have had it out with my mother when he returned home – as indeed he should have done in the first place.

It was all the more hurtful for him because, I honestly believe, he'd never slept with any other woman but my mother. Men of his generation and class – respectable Nonconformist working-class – went to their wedding-beds virgin, if only because they didn't know anything about birth control. And they generally stayed faithful because they hadn't much option. It takes money to be unfaithful, what with lunches and dinners and drinks and presents and hotel rooms, and you also need a cast-iron excuse for staying out all night. People like my father didn't have the money to spare and they didn't travel in the course of their jobs except a few miles occasionally from one wretched little town to another. A town, moreover, where everything that everyone did was watched as far as it could be watched and where there just wasn't anywhere to go. I don't maintain that it was impossible for a man in my father's circumstances to commit adultery but it was extremely difficult. And on top of that was the Nonconformist morality, which was stern and unyielding. My father didn't go to chapel any more, but the chapel morality was in his bones.

After he died no one bothered about my feelings. There was a certain amount of sympathy at school for a day or so; at least the other kids more or less stopped playing with me, except for Jeff. They wouldn't even argue with me or give me a playful shove. You'd have thought that I'd contracted something infectious. On the Monday, Miss Scott came up and sat beside me as the others were leaving the classroom, and said, 'I'm dreadfully sorry to hear about your father, Jim,' and I was aware of her closeness, the warmth which emanated from her, her wonderful female smell. What other word is there for it but wonderful, no matter how much the bitches hurt us, no matter how much they damage us? I smelled that wonderful female smell and then she took my hand, and her hand was cool, not cold, not clammy but *cool*, with long slim fingers and rosy, clean nails; near to her I could smell her breath and I'll swear it smelled sweet as a baby's – sweeter, because babies sometimes are sick. She had a blue skirt and a pale blue polo-neck sweater; the sweater wasn't tight but I could see the shape of her breasts, and her skirt was stretched tight because of the way she was sitting and I could see the outline of her suspender button, and the tingling sensation started between my legs.

I can remember that but I can't remember what I said to her, if indeed I did anything very much but mumble. It would have been better for me if I could have had a good cry, but I don't remember crying after my father's death. Crying by boys was not encouraged in my childhood, and you can say that again. I did cry at the funeral when my father's coffin was actually lowered into the grave, but not for very long. I expect that these days everyone would have made a fuss of me, and made my father's death an excuse for me whenever I behaved badly. As it was, after a week or so, it was as if nothing had happened. I'm not so sure that that isn't the best way.

My Uncle Sidney never came to the house alone again, but always with my Auntie Emma and the kids. My mother was not visibly ravaged by grief; doubtless she would rather have not had my father die, but she very quickly adapted herself to widowhood. My father had been well insured and the house was now hers; a month after he died she got a job in the largest of two hairdressing salons in the town, and Aunt Ada took care of me, coming in the afternoon to make my tea and baby-sitting when necessary. My mother seemed to work late quite a lot and went out at least twice a week; she learned to drive the Austin, but she had a positive genius for discovering boy friends who had their own transport.

I worked all this out afterwards. I cannot be sure how much of it I was aware of at the time. I'm absolutely positive that my mother started to put it about like mad as soon as she was widowed, and has continued to do so right up till now and will never stop as long as she has the strength to open her legs. But as long as I was there she didn't put it about in our house. Perhaps she had a superstitious feeling that, if she did, another death would be the result. More likely she knew that Auntie Ada wouldn't stand for it, and she needed Auntie Ada too much ever to go against her.

Why didn't my mother marry again? She had her own house and a good job – later she took over the salon – she was by any standards a good-looking woman, and one boy is no great impediment. I believe that the simple answer is that she liked her freedom too much. She may of course have been punishing herself for what she did to my father, but in my experience people just don't do things like that. My father may have had a Nonconformist conscience; she certainly didn't. I don't remember her ever talking about my father. He was hardly cold in the ground before she gave all his clothes to the Salvation Army; and even before the War had ended she had begun the process of redecoration and refurnishing which was eventually to rid the house of all visible traces of his existence. I don't know why she didn't move; I would have done in her place. But that's silly; no woman would ever be influenced by the same considerations as a man. I think that they're a different species – possibly even a higher species – and we can only judge them as dogs judge humans, according to whether they kick or caress us.

Looking back I remember Flight-Lieutenant Stanwyck best, and perhaps that was only because of his MG Midget. He was a smallish young man with a large sandy RAF moustache, rather nervous in his manner, and with the first genuine public-school accent that I'd ever heard. It must have been the summer after my father's death; I remember that I was eating blackberry-and-apple pie when the front door bell rang.

My mother was upstairs in the bathroom; it had been her afternoon off. There was a smell of geranium bath-salts coming down the stairs.

'Answer the door!' my mother yelled.

I opened the door to see Flight-Lieutenant Stanwyck. He had a bunch of roses in his hand and his face was sunburned.

'Hello, old chap,' he said. 'Tell Mummy I'm here, will you?'

I let him in without saying anything and showed him into the sitting-room. At that stage it was still the best room, not to be used for everyday occasions, but already the original wallpaper had been replaced by a pink and white striped pattern and the suite had pink and white loose covers in a floral pattern.

Flight-Lieutenant Stanwyck sat down in the nearest armchair and pulled out a packet of Gold Flake. 'Do you think your Mummy would object if I had a gasper, old chap?'

I shook my head. He tapped the cigarette end on his thumb-nail and lit the cigarette, blowing out a succession of smoke rings, something which people don't seem to do any more. He kept looking about the room with short jerky movements of his head, and his left leg kept jerking, as if of its own accord. He saw me looking at him and put his legs together with his left hand on his left knee.

'Are you a fighter pilot?' I asked him.

'Bombers,' he said, and grimaced. 'Every night when the weather's good, and sometimes when it isn't, we rain down bombs on the wicked Nazis. Men, women, and children, old chap.' He took his left hand away from his knee and started to tap with his fingers on the chair arm as if sending Morse.

'What kind of aeroplane do you fly?'

'Airplane, old chap. Lancasters, actually.' His left leg began to twitch again.

'Have you been on a lot of missions?'

'Bad form to talk about it.' He smiled. He had very white teeth which obviously were his own. I was used to seeing grown-ups with false teeth. 'Frankly, old chap, I don't care if I never see an airplane again.'

My mother came into the room in a pink satin dressing-gown, her black shining hair down to her shoulders. Even I could see that she looked extraordinarily young.

'Hello, Sam darling,' she said. 'I'll be a few minutes yet.'

His left leg stopped twitching. His face seemed suddenly extremely young and helpless, the moustache an accessory for a children's fancy-dress party. 'That's all right, Val. Your son is entertaining me.'

She pointed towards the sideboard. 'Help yourself to a drink.'

His gaze followed her out of the room. He looked at me, slightly embarrassed.

'I tell you what,' he said, 'I'll take you for a spin in my little bus. Would you like that?'

I nodded. That's another difference between then and now. Although we had a car, I didn't ride in it very much. A car ride was still a *joyride*, not just transportation. And the MG had enormous glamour, with cycle-type wings, bonnet strap, cut-away sides, slab-sided petrol tank and its general air of jaunty masculinity. I don't suppose that it was very fast – perhaps seventy with a following wind – but it looked and sounded fast and even smelled fast – oil and leather and petrol – and, inside, the large Jaeger dials, particularly the rev counter, gave the sensation of danger and adventure. It was more like an aeroplane cockpit than the interior of a car; one couldn't imagine it ever making a prosaic, necessary journey.

The Flight-Lieutenant grinned at me as I clambered in beside him. The windscreen was folded down and the small aero screen up, which added to the pleasure and the sensation of speed even though the highest speed we attained was sixty in a short burst on the road outside the town, a narrow but straight road bordered by moorland. But sixty in those days was a significant speed, a mile a minute, and at the age of seven sitting beside a RAF pilot with the wind stinging my face, old enough to be aware that the MG was a car which had to be *driven* every second, in which you had to make allowances for every bump in the road, for every tiny variation of direction, the steering being so sensitive and high-geared, the springing being so hard, it was an incomparably more intense sensation than a hundred and ten in the Granada, in which in any case sixty is merely a comfortable cruising speed and the only problem is keeping awake on a long journey.

All this is important. I wouldn't remember it if it weren't. For there was tangled inextricably with the pleasure of the ride the recollection of how my mother had looked when she'd come downstairs in her pink satin dressing-gown and Flight-Lieutenant Stanwyck's reaction. She had seemed smaller, softer, a different person, a person she had no business to be; she'd stolen somebody else's body, or someone else had stolen her body; she wasn't my mother any longer, but Flight-Lieutenant Stanwyck's solace, like the Gold Flake he lit up when we returned to the house or the rum and orange he helped himself to when he settled down to wait for her.

Now pouring myself a large Scotch, I'm aware that I have to be careful. There are two ways to go. I have been there before at least once a week over the past three years.

There is the first way, the easiest way: another large Scotch with plenty of ice, and another, sipped very slowly. The Scotch has to be taken very slowly; time has to be killed. On her night out she never stays out past midnight. There was no formal agreement between us; that's simply how it's happened. Perhaps she thinks that what she does on her night out doesn't count as adultery until after midnight. The Scotches taken slowly enable me not to think about her being out, or at least to believe her cover story. I now accept her cover story without comment. It's generally a pretty perfunctory sort of story – keeping a neighbour's wife company when her husband's away on business, going to see her old friend Myrtle in Isleworth, visiting another friend in hospital, always a London hospital, playing squash, attending a meeting of our Amenities Association or the local consumers' group or our Literary Society or our Film Society. It has to be an acceptable and reasonable story; wherever she goes must be somewhere where I wouldn't want to go, and where eyebrows wouldn't be raised if she went by herself. The only time when the cover story's entirely true is when she goes out with Cliff Droylsden. I don't know why this is the exception to the rule; I suspect that the reason is to keep me in my place. Cliff wouldn't dream of anything so brutal as spelling out what got me where I am; but it would give Sheila great pleasure.

I accept it. Some nights – this is the second way – I stop at one lager. I may read or look at the TV or listen to gramophone records or do something useful about the house. There have been nights when I've been a trifle irritated by her coming in, because I've wanted to continue what I was doing. If you spend the whole working day racing against time, making a hundred decisions which, if they're wrong, will be used as ammunition against you, and not in the distant future either, it's wonderfully soothing to be by yourself. I don't like people all that much – I find them interesting, but then so do I find piranha, and adders, and hyenas interesting. Alone I can walk round my *white* town, my *shining* town, add to its amenities – a brightly-painted roundabout in the park, a fountain in a little square, a new festival just for the hell of it, as an excuse for processions and fancy dress and fireworks – and I can get to know its people better.

That's good, that's very good, that's sustaining, that heals my pride. But the whisky way can lead to self-pity and to anger. I have gone beyond three, gone on to six and seven and eight; I've actually packed an overnight bag and written a note to Sheila. Just: *I can't stand it any more, J.* No more, because there is no need to tell her what I feel. I've made it plain enough more than once, although of course I haven't made it plain why I've stood it for so long, why I've accepted the ritual of the cover story. That is the secret I keep from her and from everyone else, the reason why I married her, the reason why I tear up the note and unpack the overnight bag. And then I drink strong coffee and drink soda-water and even then feel lousy the morning after. I go to work, nevertheless, because it doesn't do to give the impression of poor health – the piranha, so to speak, smell the blood.

But recently I've come to dislike the arrangement. I'd almost rather that she said right out that the purpose of her evening was a skinful of booze and a rousing fuck. The unquestioning acceptance of the cover story is the more civilised way – it's just that it's all too civilised, it smells of corruption. There is another stage that we could reach, that very occasionally she's hinted at, after dinner at the coffee and brandy stage, lightly, jokingly – *We're missing out, darling. We're not taking full advantage of the*

Permissive Society – and then the leg-show which she knows I can't resist, then rising, moving over to me and, very lightly, stroking my prick, then back to her chair and more leg-show and the low husky voice, the light unconcerned tone – *Marcia shook me rigid last night . . . She told me that she and Dudley, mind you, he's a little goat . . . Well, Jane and Karl popped in late one night, and they got a bit pissed without meaning to and then it all happened . . .* Her tongue moistening her lips, her legs apart for a moment. I know Marcia and Dudley and Jane and Karl, and I've been to Marcia's and Dudley's house, a huge sham-Elizabethan house with ten bedrooms and six bathrooms and a minstrel's gallery and separate staff quarters, and I can well imagine what happened, the naked romps given an extra *frisson* by the thick carpeting and heavy dark furniture and oak panelling and tapestries and suits of armour; and Sheila continued, her tone still amused, but a little excited now – *Dudley says Jane has a super figure under those WVS outfits she wears, firm as a sixteen-year-old and she's nearly forty . . .*

What did I say? Not very much. I just listened; there wasn't any need for me to talk. I was visualising Jane with her fresh round face, Marcia with her dark thin face with the full lips, a gypsyish face. I was visualising Jane undressing, and it would be precisely her WVS outfit that would turn me on, the sensible shoes and heavy denier tights, the tweed skirt and jacket or the woolly twin set. *What happened, then?* I asked, trying to keep my tone light. *A swap, what else? Mind you, I'm sure they've done it privately, if you see what I mean . . . They're the end, they really are . . . Tell you something else, too.* And she moistened her lips again. *Marcia went on far more about Jane than she did about Karl . . .*

I think that I said that that was rather sick, in fact the whole damned thing was, and Sheila shrugged her shoulders and agreed with me and the subject was dropped, but that evening I realised something which I should have realised long before, that if you become addicted to strong tastes, if you like your game high and your cheese strong, you're always looking for even stronger tastes. Sheila sent up a trial balloon that evening, of that I'm convinced. I don't think that it was an issue of great concern to her but if I'd indicated that I'd be actively interested I believe that plans would have been made, not cut-and-dried plans, but plans half in joke, and I'd have been drawn into her little circle, or rather her huge circle, and people like Jane and Karl would have sooner or later dropped into my home late at night for a drink. And about one thing I am determined: the only sexual activity in our house will be what takes place between Sheila and me behind a locked bedroom door, and nothing else will take place that isn't fit for Gareth and Sharon to see. And I make the pronouncement, a sane and solid decision, and Sheila accepts it because by and large she has what she wants and values what she has; and I know, having tried it briefly, that I wouldn't be happy in Sheila's circle, not so much for reasons of morality but reasons of taste, of fastidiousness. But if Sheila wants something she generally gets it; I've never told her my secret, I've never told anyone my secret, but she knows that she has me by the balls if ever a woman had. And if ever she does desire even stronger tastes, the real corruption, she might draw me in too. I'm old enough to know that the one thing you swear you'll never do is what you wake up to find yourself doing.

No, no Master, I'll never betray you. I'm surprised you should say that, Lord. You've really hurt me. I didn't expect it from you. I thought you loved me. I honestly believed you loved me. I'd put my hand in the fire for you, Lord, I really would. I'd be happy to die for you – And not long after here's Peter again, his hands in his pockets or wherever they put them in those days, trying to look like a passer-by, mildly curious about the hubbub, whistling to indicate his complete unconcern, sweating a bit, though it's turned cool – *Who, me? Are you talking to me? Good God, no, of course I don't know Him. Seen Him around, making trouble and doing conjuring-tricks, that's all. No, no, I wouldn't touch the sod with a bargepole. Maybe you saw someone who looked like me. Not that I'm flattered if you've mixed me up with one of those loonies. Frankly, if He's in the shit now, it serves Him right –*

What use is it to weep afterwards, you face against the cold stone of the courtyard wall, your guts churned up and a rotten taste in your mouth, the sound of the cock crowing hurting your ears? What use would it be for me to weep, waking with a hangover with, very likely, a strange woman in the bed, remembering the tangle of naked bodies, the moaning and writhing and the smell of semen and sweat and perfume and booze, the couples attacking each other like enemies, the moaning and the screaming and the high-pitched giggles? And Gareth or Sharon, half awake, looking without comprehension but with horror, real horror, horror that will follow them all through their lives, twist and warp and cripple them? Without comprehension? Without immediate and full comprehension in the *front* of their minds, but with immediate and full comprehension *deep down* in their minds, immediate and full, but wrong, totally and utterly wrong because it's too much, an adult-size burden on a child's shoulders. Who knows this better than me?

And this is what happens when you hold nothing back. You get more than you bargained for, you're tormented not only by what actually happened but also by what hasn't happened yet. And yet I go on, sprawling on the sofa now, sipping the Scotch. I can't take the extraction without anaesthetics, though I know what the anaesthetics will do to me afterwards; the nagging headache, the swelling sensation inside the mouth, the persistent nausea then gradually the ache and the depression. But I have to go on, wrench out the roots, and it's too much to bear without the Scotch, the gradual easing of the crunching disrupting pain, *pressing down*, *pressing down*, the way in which clothes, furniture, the weather outside, the smell of violets and geraniums and the inside of the MG can all accumulate, swarm together into a lynch mob – *Christ, I nearly came.* No, I did not understand the words themselves, for me at seven to come was simply to move, to arrive at Point A from Point B. Yes, I did understand, because the understanding was programmed into me before I was born. But the button was pressed too soon.

I think of Aunt Ada, so I can leave the Scotch alone and light a cigarette. I have no memories of Aunt Ada that hurt. She is the reason why I'm not in a worse mess, why I've kept out of the hands of the psychiatrists and the police, why I am General Manager of Droylsden's, a husband and a father and not on drugs, alcohol, or tranquillisers. She was a staunch though not fanatical Methodist and her beliefs were black and white, with no nonsense about tolerance and seeing good in both sides. She was actually my great-aunt on my father's side, but great-aunt is a term more often used by the middle classes than the working classes, God knows why. Since she was our only relative in the town and my mother wasn't a very neighbourly kind of woman, she was absolutely indispensable; and until I left home none of my mother's boy friends ever spent a night in the house. They didn't even call very often: Aunt Ada had ways of making them uncomfortable.

97

On the day that Flight-Lieutenant Stanwyck came to our house I remember with great pleasure seeing her in action. She came in carrying a large basket and wearing a voluminous fawn macintosh and a red babuska scarf which made her bony face seem especially grim. She nodded at my mother, brushed my cheek with her lips, frowned at Lieutenant Stanwyck, who, astoundingly, blushed and disappeared into the kitchen. I followed her, to find her taking off the macintosh, revealing a severe, high-necked black wool dress, its only embellishment a large cameo brooch. The rubbery, rather melancholy smell of the macintosh filled the kitchen for a moment.

'He took me for a ride in his MG, Auntie,' I told her.

'As long as he's sober, that's all right,' she said.

'He flies bombers,' I said. 'His name's Flight-Lieutenant Stanwyck.'

'That's san fairy ann to me. I see your mother's using the best room again. She'll make it a proper tip soon.'

My mother and Flight-Lieutenant Stanwyck appeared at the door of the kitchen. 'We're off now, Auntie,' my mother said. She had on a squirrel coat and was wearing a red babuska too, but it did things for her face, with its bright eyes and red lips, that it didn't do for Aunt Ada. 'This is Flight-Lieutenant Stanwyck, by the way.' It was evident that she relished introducing an officer.

Aunt Ada stared at him coldly and he blushed again.

'Pleased to meet you,' she said. 'You look very young. What do you do when you're not bombing people?'

Flight-Lieutenant Stanwyck looked at the ground. 'I help my Papa run his estates, actually. Not very well, I'm afraid.'

'I hope you drive that contraption outside very well. This little lad's only got her, and I won't live for ever.' She sniffed. 'Two things are a curse for young men, my father used to say. Drink and older women.'

'A short life and a merry one,' Flight-Lieutenant Stanwyck said, recovering himself.

'Aye, I've heard people say that.' She sighed. 'Don't be too late,' she said to my mother. 'And don't let him drink too much.'

My mother smiled; at least, her lips forced themselves into a grimace which was meant to be a smile, but her eyes were angry. 'Don't worry, Auntie. I'll drive if necessary.' She kissed me on the cheek; her lips were very soft. 'Bye-bye, Jim, and do exactly what your Auntie Ada tells you. Bye-bye, Ada.'

Flight-Lieutenant Stanwyck smiled at Auntie Ada. It was a genuine smile. But he was not comfortable. I don't know how he wasn't comfortable, but he wasn't in the same mood as when he entered the house. 'Good-night,' he said. 'Very nice to have met you.' He bent down to me and shook my hand, leaving half a crown in it. 'Good night, old chap. I'll take you a longer ride next time.'

He didn't, of course. About a month later he went down in flames over the Ruhr. My mother heard about it from another pilot at the same bomber station and told me about it quite casually. With all her many faults, she was never a hypocrite. I doubt if she shed a tear for him. I remember him because he was one of the few who ever entered the house when Aunt Ada was there and, I expect, because there was something rather innocent and childish about him. No, that's sentimental nonsense; it was the ride in the MG which made him stick in my mind.

I didn't spend all my waking hours during childhood agonising over my mother's putting it about. I adapted, as most of us do. I would have liked a father, though I wouldn't have liked my mother to marry again; what I wanted was a sort of instant package deal with a *father* and a *mother* – settled, middle-aged, apparently sexless, their sole function being to look after me. For my mother to have married one of her boy friends would have been totally unsatisfactory, since she'd have only done it to please herself. Worst of all, it would have been somehow connected with my secret pleasure, would have been its public revelation, its shameful externalisation.

I never believed that it would make me blind or mad because I knew that all other boys did it, from which I reasoned that all men must have done it. It remained a solitary pleasure; as I grew older it was always stimulated by mental pictures of girls, never girls whom I had actually seen, but pin-ups, photos and drawings indiscriminately. Jeff and I each had a secret store, mine under a heap of old tiles in the garden shed, his under a loose floorboard in his bedroom, which we used to swap. The best one was discovered by Jeff in a pile of old *Picture Posts* – the girl on the Giant Caterpillar with her skirt blowing up to show her suspenders and slip. She's a very pretty blonde, she has a happy face, she's screaming with laughter, and she's a private person, she's *real*. God bless her, whoever she was; she gave me hours of pleasure. It amused me to discover recently that in the original she's showing her knickers; Jeff and I often used to speculate about that, because we couldn't fathom how she could avoid it, and came to the conclusion that she mustn't have been wearing any, which made the photo still more enjoyable. But this was the star item in our collections, better even than the very few nudes we'd managed to obtain. The trouble with the nudes was that the photographers were so intent upon proving that they were artists and not pornographers that what they produced in the end was a representation of a statue, not of a naked woman. Even a clipping from an underwear advertisement was more realistic because whoever drew it must have had some recollection of a real woman in his head, and it showed.

I am still putting it off. I still don't want to think about it; its beginning to hurt. I need the anaesthetic and I put out my cigarette and light another and I finish the whisky off and pour myself another, a double double, and go into the kitchen and put in more ice, and lie on the sofa again, sipping the whisky slowly, despising myself for needing it.

I cannot even remember how old I was when I made the discovery; I should think about eleven or twelve. Jeff and I were sharing a cubicle at the municipal swimming baths because we were talking about football and didn't wish to break off the conversation. Suddenly he glanced at me.

'Gosh, what a little prick you have. It's *tiny* –' Then he stopped. 'It'll grow,' he said.

But I'd looked at his, something I'd never done before, the only penis I was interested in being my own. And his was at least three times longer and thicker. That's all I remember about the details, and if I drank a whole bottle of whisky it wouldn't make any difference. I put on my costume – it was a costume with a top; trunks were seldom worn then, even by little boys – as quickly as possible and from that day onward never let anyone see me naked. That is, any man. For if there's a pokeable woman around it grows to a respectable length of six inches and a respectable thickness too. (I measured the length once but when I got down to measuring the thickness I burst out laughing and the erection subsided.)

I've learned to cope with this, and if the worst came to the worst and a man saw it, there's always one perfect answer: the test of the rider is in the saddle. And, after all, one isn't all that different from most male animals; if the penis of a bull or a stallion were the same size quiescent as when erect, they wouldn't survive very long as a species, for obvious reasons. It doesn't matter now; but it did matter very much that day at the baths. I can still smell that cubicle – chlorine and stale sweat and wet wood – still feel the slats of the platform under my feet, still see the grey stone walls and green canvas curtain, still hear the voices from the pool echoing, echoing, somehow desolate, still feel the hatred and shame. I suppose it helped to further mess me up; needless to say, there was no one to whom I could take the problem. Which is just as well: a problem shared is a problem doubled, because the sort of do-good creeps to whom you take the problem both dominate you and make you feel rather a splendid chap just because you're unfortunate. But there was no danger of that happening to me at that time in that town. You just had to bite the bullet, get on or go under.

That is out now, and don't think it doesn't still hurt. You can't remember physical pain – or at least I can't – but you can remember that sort of pain. Although to all intents and purposes I've recovered, yet to this day I can find myself for no reason at all suddenly hating my body, seeing it as a lice-crawling corpse inescapably enveloping me, dirty and disease-ridden. And at those moments I want to burn it off me, be clean again and rid of shame. It passes; everything passes if you expect no help from anybody, if you bit the bullet, if you *endure*.

Endure: I speak the word aloud. The parquet floor, the teak bureau, dark with a rich glint of red, the colour almost of strong tea, the walnut cocktail-cabinet, the white and orange wall unit, chosen by Sheila, which I thought was a mistake but which is perfect because the colours are picked up by the white and orange curtains and the white and orange loose covers on the sofa – these help almost as much as the whisky. The door is full-length glass, which doesn't help me at all, since I'm always worrying about Gareth or Sharon running into it. Now I look away towards the TV cabinet, the doors closed now, looking like a large Jacobean-style chest in dark oak. It isn't like a TV set at all, which I'm all for, because I hate the gibbering blankness of a TV screen when not switched on, but Sheila bought it from Harrod's and I could have got her something nearly as good at half the price. We had one of our infrequent rows about that; I like the best, the very best, as much as anyone, but I can't bear paying full price. Now the temptation is to make it into a TV, to lie on the sofa and let the water go over my head, even though, now that I need oblivion, what I shall get will be a documentary on starving tea-plantation workers or violence in Northern Ireland or something equally boring. Another whisky, though, and I can enjoy even programmes of this nature in a horrid sort of way, reflecting woozily that whatever my troubles at least I'm not starving or being blown up or shot at. But it's no use; I'm not going to look at TV, or listen to gramophone records, or read – the probe is going to go deep again, it's all going to be wrenched out, and I hold the probe and I am the patient. I tell the patient that this won't hurt, and despite the cocaine the patient knows damned well it will –

Lorraine. Like Sandra or Shirley or Lindsey or Samantha or, come to that, my mother's name Valerie, a dead give-away, a name once fashionable then discarded and grabbed by show business, discarded by show business and grabbed by the working classes, who see it in their innocence as a name with real class, a touch of glamour, not realising that what was gold leaf is now merely gilt, and tarnished at that. Lorraine, who was a clever girl who, despite her left-wing tendencies, was chiefly activated by the burning desire to get the hell out of the working classes, has probably changed it to Laura or Liz by now.

I met her in my first year at university. I'm not really an academic type – I like *things* more than ideas – but at that period they were shoving everyone through to higher education who could read and write, and even some who couldn't. And the proprietor of the hairdressing salon where my mother worked had retired and my mother bought the salon, with the help of a boy friend named Henry. Henry was a solicitor in his late fifties: he was a cut above her usual run, white-haired, immaculate without effort or ostentation, cool and unemotional in his manner, with a beautifully enunciated voice. I have to remember him now, because I have to remember Lorraine. I only met him once, very briefly; it was he who pointed out to my mother that in the future a degree would be indispensable to get a decent job. And my mother, in one of the rare moments when she thought about anyone except herself, agreed with him, and pushed me in my last two years at the grammar school. She probably reasoned also that it would be a feather in her cap to have a son at the university. The general image of students in those days was of brilliant high-spirited lads without an ounce of harm in them; in fact they were never called students but undergraduates, a bit wild perhaps, but fundamentally sound, scholars and gentlemen. I can't remember meeting either at the Department of Economics at my university, but it was not my ambition to become either. I did in fact get rid of my Lancashire accent and learn the basics of middle-class manners and dress and so on; but I knew very well that nothing could make me a gentleman. Or an economist either; but I got a reasonable degree and, as the saying goes, you can take me anywhere.

There's no point in remembering the university. It was new, mainly in concrete, absolutely the wrong material for that area, and hideous. The nearest town was five miles away and it was just as depressing as my hometown. I might have felt differently about it if I'd been in residence there, but someone had miscalculated about the accommodation needed, so I lived at home. I had a second-hand Hillman Minx then, so travel was no great hardship. My story is a love story, not a rags-to-riches story. The town I lived in certainly wasn't permissive. It did have permissive areas, if you knew the password; but the sojourners in those areas, even my mother, kept their mouths shut about it in public. It was rigidly and strictly moral. But the value of money stayed the same from year to year and it definitely was affluent, even in Lancashire.

The probe isn't in use yet. As always, I'm a coward. The patient is ready, trembling a bit, holding the arms of the chair rather too tightly, but I know that he won't bolt out of the room. What the probe is going to do, it should have done a long time ago; he's put it off too often. Don't wash your hands again, don't ask him again if his mouth is really numb, don't talk about the weather. *Get on with it.*

Lorraine had light brown hair and a round face. She had large blue eyes and a fair complexion. She was tall – about five foot seven – and had good teeth. Her legs were rather too sturdy, the ankles a hair's-breadth from being thick; they looked best in high-heeled shoes. She had a big bottom, but I didn't mind that, in fact rather liked it. Her breasts weren't big, but they were adequate. They would have seemed more than adequate if she'd worn an uplift bra and tighter blouses and sweaters; but at that time that would have been considered vulgar. So would décolleté except for evening wear.

Jeff introduced me to her in the Students' Union bar one Saturday evening. Jeff was reading English and was into the Labour Group and the Drama Group and even various good works, so I didn't see so much of him those days. We were still friends, but we were beginning to go in different directions. After the introduction I bought Jeff a pint of bitter and her half a pint of mild and asked her again what she was reading (I'd already been told by Jeff that it was English) and grumbled about the draught in the bar and said it was more like December than September (it was wet and windy with an overcast sky and had been so for three weeks) and asked her what she had in mind after graduation. I really would have liked not to have talked at all but just have sat and looked at her; she wasn't a raving beauty but she was a pokeable girl, perhaps even the girl to whom I would lose my virginity.

Whether she was a virgin or not I didn't know; and I hadn't had enough experience to be able to tell. If she wasn't, she was in a minority. To tell the truth, I hoped she wasn't, because I had a rather daunting vision of the hymen as being a barrier it needed a hammer and chisel to penetrate. In the meantime I was quite happy simply to talk with Lorraine and to imagine what she was like under her clothes. *Imagine* is the key word: at the age of twenty I had never seen a naked woman. The photographs of nudes which I had seen, mainly in the nudist magazine *Health and Efficiency* (and what on earth does efficiency have to do with it?), were so heavily airbrushed as to give the impression that women's nipples were sharply-pointed with a circle of smooth dark flesh round them, that they had no pubic hair, and that the genitals were completely hidden between the legs. I did know the true facts from what Jeff had told me, but I didn't really believe him. Or perhaps I didn't want to believe him. Anyway, I hadn't had much experience beyond kissing girls I'd picked up at dances, and even a kiss in those days was regarded as a great privilege. There used to be articles solemnly debating whether a girl should allow a boy to kiss her on her first date; the general opinion was that she should get to know him first. And people used to talk a lot about falling in love, which I consider now to be rather touching, agreeably innocent – why on earth shouldn't sex be dressed up a bit?

At some point in the evening we were joined by Audrey, another girl from the English department. For Jeff and I were still at the stage where we took girls out as a foursome.

Lorraine smoked; everyone did then. I offered her a Churchman's Number One; they were fat cigarettes in a green packet, more expensive than the ordinary size. She opened her eyes wide, a trick of hers. 'Oh, aren't we posh!' she said. She was at the first stage of Standard English, exaggerating a little: the *oh* came out as *oah* and the *posh* had a little too much emphasis. My mother, under the influence of Henry, had passed that stage; but I remembered it and took it for granted that she should be doing her best to speak properly.

'Jim's mother is a bloated capitalist,' Jeff said. 'Keeps a hairdresser's salon.'

'*My* old man's a dustman,' she said. 'Like the song.'

'I'm afraid my father's a bank manager,' Audrey said rather coldly. She was a thin dark-haired girl in a rather fussy blue woollen dress with a white collar and cuffs. 'Another bloated capitalist.'

'He looks after other people's capital,' I said. 'That's an important distinction.'

'He's the servant of capital,' Lorraine said. 'He helps to perpetuate inequality.'

I'm sure she talked like that. We all did at university in those days. I mean that we were all articulate and reasonably grammatical and tried to make ourselves clear. Though very little of what I learned at the university has been of any practical use to me, I did at least learn that much. And the way in which Lorraine talked increased my excitement by the minute: it wasn't her ideas which I liked but the way in which she expressed them.

When she had spoken she gave me a searching look. I know now that it wasn't a look of sexual but of financial appraisal; but I thought then, God help me, that she was quite simply attracted to me.

'You appear to disapprove,' she said. 'You're not a Tory, are you?'

'Good God, no!' In my hometown no one of my age-group admitted to being a Tory. 'It's just that I'm not terribly interested in politics.'

'And you're an economist!' she said indignantly, her eyes opening wide again. 'You ought to be ashamed of yourself!' It was as if I'd personally insulted her.

'You'll have to convert me,' I said.

'Jim's a hard case,' Jeff said lightly. 'He's not in the least concerned with the unfairness of the system, merely with extracting the most he can for himself out of it.'

'Aren't we all?' Audrey said.

'No, we're not!' Lorraine burst out. 'Some of us want to make it work better; some of us want to build a just society –'

That is how it went at first; I didn't argue with her very much because it wasn't her ideas that I was interested in. Young though I was I did know that you can't go very far wrong if you appear to be actively listening; so I appeared as if I was actively listening. I'd heard most of it before from Jeff, and he knew that I didn't agree with any of it, so it was no use pretending to; but I didn't passionately disagree with any of it either, so I couldn't give her a run for her money. I just didn't care; even then I had a shrewd idea that in this world you either screw or are screwed, and I didn't intend to be screwed. I wanted to know *how* the system worked, and that was all. And that was difficult enough, without attempting to change it. The only thing I wanted to change right then was my status as virgin.

Two pints later we moved to the Seven Bells on the outskirts of Knutsford. That was another difference in those days: you never worried overmuch about drinking and driving. As long as you could actually walk to the car without assistance you were considered fit to drive. Once in the car, I was amused to note, Lorraine, who'd been dominating the conversation, turned quiet. Politics were theory; the Minx was reality. Though it was second-hand it was in good shape, and my mother had it regularly maintained for me, and well maintained since she took great pains with the hair of the garage proprietor's wife and gave her a discount on make-up and scent and other things.

'Daddy has one of these,' Audrey said. I noticed again that she didn't have to sweat with her accent as Lorraine did.

'The bloody thing knows its own way to the Seven Bells by now,' Jeff said. 'Why don't we go into the town and then have fish and chips at Sweaty Betty's?'

'The girls wouldn't like any of the pubs in the town,' I said. This was quite true: the pubs in the town had as their only female habitués old-age pensioners, grim and shapeless middle-aged matrons, and the occasional scrubber. They were more like Scottish pubs than English pubs, dark and dingy places in which the only thing to do was to get pissed out of your mind.

'I thought that Lorraine was proud to have come out of the working classes,' Jeff said. 'I thought she was part of the great throbbing heart of the working classes.' He'd got in an extra pint before leaving and was in a rather aggressive mood. 'There's dustmen and navvies and weavers and miners in the pubs in the town. Miners. Like my old grandad, bless him. Salt of the earth.'

'Oh God!' Audrey said, 'he's going to start talking about blood on the coal next.'

I laughed; I was beginning to like Audrey. I've often wondered what my life would have been like if I'd been with her instead of Lorraine.

'The miners go to their clubs,' I said. 'As you know damned well.'

'Alienation,' Lorraine said. 'People forced apart. Alienation . . . This is more comfortable than the bus . . .' Her eyes were half closed. That was before everyone had cars. She probably could have counted on her fingers the number of times she'd ridden in one. A few others at the university had cars; but not many. Unquestionably, the Minx had put me a move ahead.

'The Seven Bells is bourgeois,' said Jeff. 'Pretentious, bogus, *bourgeois*.' It was a word which he used at every opportunity.

'Who cares?' I said. 'Get to know your enemy. Mark them down for liquidation.'

The rain had stopped and the high wind had scrubbed

the sky clean of clouds except for a few wisps caught around the moon. The sky was a genuine indigo; just here, if nowhere else, there was little smoke. The road from the university was new and raw with heaps of newly-dug earth on the verges. Beyond the verges was flat featureless grassland. In the light of the headlamps the grass had a black tinge. No houses, no trees, no cows, no sheep, no buses, flat featureless grassland under the moon, and the heater on in the car bringing out the smell of leather and tobacco and beer and face-powder and above all the girls, the clean healthy girls with naked bodies under their clothes; my erection came with startling suddenness

Young girls were more feminine then; this makes me sound old, but it's absolutely true. They wore fully-fashioned stockings and high heels and skirts, and when they were being taken out they'd take special pains and wash and brush their hair till it shone, shone softly, blew over their eyes and across your face, the clouds caught by the moon, the great visible difference between the sexes. Men wore their hair short and, particularly if they were undergraduates, went in for tweeds and stout shoes. I was wearing a collar-attached brown and yellow checked Viyella shirt with a yellow woollen tie and a Windsor knot, a fawn thornproof tweed suit and brown Lotus brogues; Jeff had a blue checked Harris tweed jacket and dark blue slacks and a plain blue shirt and the university tie in blue and gold, and black casuals. We were both very interested in clothes and he had thought a great deal about the shoes in particular, feeling that black went best with blue but that brown was best with a tweed sports jacket. Today, I suppose, we'd have all worn jeans and cheesecloth shirts and the girls' hair might well have been shorter than the boys'.

'Aren't you interested in politics in the least?' Lorraine asked me. 'You sound terribly cynical to me.'

'I'm interested in you,' I said. 'You're real.'

'There's a war on,' she said.

I could see the curve of her breast very sharply for a second; I longed to touch it.

'I'm neutral,' I said. 'Strictly neutral.'

'I'm surprised you didn't read Political Science,' Audrey said sharply from the back.

'If you learn how to use words you don't need Political Science,' Lorraine said.

'No use trying to change Jim,' Jeff said. 'He loves the Affluent Society. Proper old sensualist he is.'

'Yes, *please*,' Audrey said, and giggled, and even Lorraine giggled, and all of a sudden the atmosphere was exactly as it should be; we were a little high, elevated, full of wonder at our good luck, the whole world before us and any amount of choices, and the miracle of quick motion through the moonlight and the miracle of our different sexes making it a moment we'd all remember later on; we were all wide-eyed at the shop window of the future, blissfully certain that the money would arrive to buy us our choice.

Even the Seven Bells, a huge red-brick building surrounded by a car park, was part of that window display. It had been built in 1938 when someone realised that there was a middle class who liked to go out with their wives and girl friends, and it had grown more and more prosperous since the working class started to acquire cars too; the car park, too large in 1938, was even now still adequate.

We went into the Cocktail Bar, where the drinks cost more but you got bowls of peanuts and cheese biscuits and olives and crisps and pickled onions; it was a 1938 décor with fluted wall lights and a zig-zag orange and green fitted carpet and tubular steel furniture which was more comfortable than it looked and an angular black and white and silver and gold mural on the wall facing the bar with 1938 characters wining, dining, dancing, playing tennis, swimming, golfing, skiing, riding, driving racing cars, but not, significantly, hunting or shooting or playing polo. For these three sports were what the customers of the Cocktail Bar wouldn't even be able to imagine themselves playing. The other two walls were in what used to be termed a futuristic pattern of gold and silver and orange; it was by then looking rather the worse for wear, but we weren't at the age to notice. I called in at the Cocktail Bar when last I was in the neighbourhood; it's been entirely redecorated and refurnished now – strictly traditional with oak panelling and oak furniture and hunting prints and plain red carpeting and very nice and cosy too, but I shall always think of it as it was, nearly full that evening of the middle classes of Knutsford – or rather of whatever middle-class people there were around Knutsford. For the Seven Bells was really a roadhouse, and the whole *raison d'être* of a roadhouse is that you must travel at least ten miles to get to it. You don't use it as a local, because it very specifically isn't a local. It's the destination of a spin, a joyride, and you should ideally travel to it in an open sports car; I'm not so sure that you shouldn't really travel to it only in the spring and the summer. (*Let's take the MG for a spin, old girl. Where shall we go, darling? Why, the Seven Bells – always a nice crowd at the Seven Bells . . .*)

I don't suppose that they were very grand, definitely not the Beautiful People or whatever they called the super-rich back in the Fifties. They'd be travellers' reps and small businessmen and rising young executives (it wasn't very

113

difficult to rise then), grammar-school rather than public-school types, their tastes running to blazers and flannels and pints and RAF moustaches and handkerchiefs in the sleeve, rather loud and hearty and jolly; if you weren't old enough to have been an officer during the war the fashion was to behave as if you would have been if you had been old enough. The girls favoured see-through blouses – though with slip and bra underneath – and high-heel shoes with ankle-straps. To me at least they seemed to radiate sexuality. There was no nonsense then about them not being sex objects. At twenty they seemed to me more than a little shocking; my touchstone of morality was still Aunt Ada rather than my mother. I was well aware that women liked sex too; but because of what I'd absorbed from those around me I was still surprised that this should be so. According to Auntie Ada all the pleasure was the man's and all the suffering the woman's; looking around me I couldn't associate any of the women there with suffering.

My erection began to trouble me; though I was also proud of it, as proud as a Heidelberg student of his new duelling scars. Afterwards – this was part of the pleasure – I should tell Jeff how randy I'd been, how much I'd wished that I'd been wearing a double-breasted suit. It is not the conversation I remember now, nor Lorraine especially, but the gleaming legs of the girls, the glimpse of stocking-top and white flesh occasionally, their high shrill voices like one voice, the 1938 mural becoming brighter-coloured as the evening went on, the figures seeming to move in the tobacco smoke, the drinks with cherries and olives and ice and lemon, and the hope growing that tonight would be the night, though I didn't really believe that anything so wonderful could happen to me.

We weren't drunk when we got into the car, though Jeff was complaining rather too loudly about the corruption of bourgeois society and its alienation from the workers, and was announcing his desire to kick in the headlights of a Jaguar 3½-litre which was parked next to us. His face looked rather too white under the flaring red hair; but I saw him take a Polo mint from his pocket, crunch it and gulp, and knew that he wouldn't be sick. Polo mints were to Jeff what spinach is to Popeye the Sailor: they saved him when all seemed lost.

'It is rather *false*, isn't it?' Lorraine said to me as I edged the Hillman out gingerly into the main road. There seemed suddenly to be a lot of fast traffic, and some of the drivers would have had far more than my five pints.

'You can go now,' Jeff said impatiently from the rear seat.

'No, I can't,' I said as a Humber Super Snipe suddenly appeared from the right, swaying and swerving at ninety, its radio blaring.

'Go on, Suicide Sid!' Jeff yelled. 'Rotten Fascist pig!'

I saw a gap and turned right. 'You take it too seriously,' I said to Lorraine. 'They're quite harmless, really.'

'Soft hands and hard hearts,' she said.

I touched her hand, then her leg, my hand feeling the outline of the suspender button. 'Our hands aren't hard, are they?'

'That's different,' she said. 'We aren't exploiting anybody.'

'It always is different,' I said. I didn't actually care what she thought: I've always assumed that in politics, as in everything else, the professionals are going to come out on top to enjoy a whacking cut off the joint with plenty of crisp fat and gravy, and seventeen years later I see no reason to change my mind. But I didn't want to quarrel with Lorraine; absurdly, some people take politics seriously. So I added in a thoughtful sincere sort of way that I did see her point and that the people in the cocktail bar were excruciatingly affected and one day I hoped that there'd be a fairer society. But what I really cared about was her smell, her female smell, clean but slightly musky now, and the curve of her breast and the curve of her cheek and the picture inside my mind of that dark secret below her waist; I was then totally woman-bedazzled, totally bewitched by the opposite sex, and I suppose that I still am.

She gave me a Woodbine, lighting it for me and putting it between my lips; it was like a signal that the serious conversation was over.

'I should have done that,' I said. 'At the wheel of my Lincoln Continental.'

'This is just as nice,' she said. 'I've enjoyed myself tonight, Jim, I really have.'

'Despite all the corrupt bourgeoisie?'

'That's part of the enjoyment too.' She put her hand on my thigh. 'You have a smashing profile,' she said. 'It's a pleasure to look at you.'

'I'm not used to compliments,' I said. 'It's a greater pleasure for me to look at you.'

'Then we're both happy,' she said. She stroked my thigh; the erection grew. A car passed with inches to spare, returning to the left-hand lane just in time to avoid a car suddenly appearing from the other direction over the brow of the hill. I turned to the right down a narrow cobbled street of terraced houses and went down a cart-track at the end where there was a small patch of open country with a hen-run and a farmhouse to the right. 'I thought we'd let the traffic quieten down a bit,' I said.

We were on the top of a small plateau with fields around us and the cart-track continuing straight down to the valley beyond a five-barred gate. It was an odd little patch of country, hemmed in by buildings; I could see the lights of the main road below. She got out of the car and I followed her down to the five-barred gate, over the stile and through a stile to the left. She walked fast despite her high heels and the rocky path, the wind blowing her hair behind her. The stone wall was waist-high; she stopped against it, looking down into the valley.

I kissed her; she returned the kiss open-mouthed, rubbing her belly against mine. Whatever happened afterwards, that will always be there. It was absolutely perfect, complete and total happiness. I closed my eyes for a moment and it was as if the breeze on my face were washing me clean, a shower of cool air, as if I were drawing into me the smell of grass and stone and earth, the feel of fine wool and nylon, the soft yet firm touch of a woman's body, so marvellously different from my own, and then I was unfastening her bra inside her sweater and felt her breasts tumble free. *Tumble* is the right word. I don't know why, because they weren't huge, they didn't flop, they'd only been braced up a little; I pulled up her sweater and she somehow arranged the shoulder-straps of her slip so that her breasts were bared and I was kissing the nipples; and that was the moment of astonishment, almost of fear, because they were larger and coarser than I had imagined. I realised that they weren't ornaments like finials on a roof, but teats, nozzles, what babies feed through, and for a split second I was within touch of understanding, had normality within my grasp, and then the idiot adolescent within me notched a little triumph on his gun-belt and the moment was still marvellous but I had missed something and, though I didn't know it then, somewhere I'd been hurt – or rather I had hurt myself. I kissed her again and moved my hand to her thigh; she gently pushed my hand away and then put her hand on my fly, unbuttoning it deftly; there was ten seconds' fumbling and then it began, acute, bitter, brutal, gasping, rough yet smooth, almost painful, an impossibly high note dragged impossibly higher, then going out, out, out, gathering in the night and the breeze and gushing, giving, very near pain now, the soft hand cupping itself around my organ, her lips drawn back over her teeth and my own voice moaning and her kissing me, her hand still on me, and a flood of warmth in my groin and an enormous sense of well-being which was the last thing I'd been led to expect.

'Oh God,' I said, 'that was super.'

'I'm glad, darling,' she said. 'Give me your hanky.'

I remember that too. That was part of it, not to be treasured any the less than the main event, the star turn of the evening; there was, too her opening her handbag and the smell of face powder – it was a very lightly-scented powder, smelling more of the schoolroom than the boudoir – and then the heavier smell of a cologne tissue, an old-fashioned smell, entirely of the boudoir this time, an indoor smell, a smell which made me think of mirrors and gilt and satin and lace bedspreads.

And afterwards, when we'd taken them back to the university hostel, it was something else; it was changed, and changed for the worse, and I can see now where I went wrong but cannot see what else I could have done.

'Wacko,' said Jeff when the girls had gone into the hostel, a large grim concrete building occupying one side of a large square. There was nothing to relieve its blankness except the huge metal abstract sculpture at the centre of the square, officially known as the Free Spirit and unofficially as the Tin Prick.

'You seem pleased with yourself,' I said as we walked through to the car park.

'Too bloody true, mate. Little Audrey has been there before. I *knew* she was hot stuff. Always the same, these refined bourgeois bitches. We were at it like knives. You'd no sooner got out of the car than she whipped out my John Thomas – mind you, I'd been touching her up all the way there. Wacko!' He leapt into the air and broke into a run; I kept on walking at the same pace.

'I presume that you also got it in,' he asked me when I'd started the car.

'Not quite,' I said. I should have told him to mind his own business, I should have kept it to myself, but for a long time now we'd been confiding these details to each other, and after he'd told me about what he'd done with Audrey, not to have told him what had happened to me would have been a breach of friendship. In some ways I'd not come anywhere near growing up. But it takes a long time to learn not to do anything that you don't want to do.

'Your technique is obviously faulty,' he said. 'Soften them up first. They daren't touch your hand when you're driving.'

'It was all right for you,' I said. 'I couldn't see you but you could see me.'

'I'll drive next time. What the hell *did* you do, anyway?'

'She tossed me off.'

'That's better than a kick up the arse, as the saying goes.'

'It was smashing. And she has gorgeous little tits.' All the time I was saying this I was aware of throwing something away, of damaging myself. No doubt Lorraine would at this moment be comparing notes with Audrey, but I knew instinctively that they'd talk in a different way, that no matter how light their tone would be they wouldn't try to disguise the fact that something important had happened, that something unique and personal had been given; they would talk like women, but we weren't talking like men. But I went on talking like an adolescent, I went on spoiling what I knew I should wrap up carefully and put away to look at when I was alone. For everything at that stage is fragile, the act of love itself is fragile, it isn't a rough and tough and *willed* act like punching someone in the jaw, and to misrepresent sex as we were misrepresenting it is to spoil it.

'Christ, she'd whipped it out for me before I knew what she was doing,' I said.

'Didn't you do anything for her? No finger pie?'

'That's when she whipped it out.'

'There might be a reason. Think hard.'

'I don't need to,' I said. The truth was that I didn't want to: menstruation was a fact of life which disgusted me, which, if I thought about it, was almost enough to put me off women entirely. I hold nothing back, even this childishness, long since outgrown, not entirely my own fault, somehow mixed up with the memory of that overheard scrap of conversation – *Christ, I nearly came* – so long ago, four bullets gone deep, the flesh around them festering. And now they're out, the flesh is healing, I accept women as they are; but that night I was mixed up, punch-drunk, I was turning a real magic, a magic to transform my world, transform it in every way, into something commonplace and shabby. I was turning the moment that soared, that drew in the air and the grass and the sense of height, that expanded, that penetrated the moon, into something earthbound, a flashily-dressed yob swaggering down mean streets; I had been near becoming an inhabitant of my *white* town, my *shining* town, and had not known it, was not to know it until now, eighteen years later, when at last I can see what I threw away. The town would have grown like a flower, like a tree, like a pool in the hollow of a rock on a high mountain; instead I've had to build it with my bare hands, stone by stone, fighting disasters all the way.

I went home to an empty house, as I generally did on a Saturday night. My mother would return in the small hours, if not on Sunday morning, generally at about eleven, cheerful but faintly bedraggled. She very rarely had a hangover; hangovers on Sunday lead to hairs-of-the-dog on Monday, and when you're self-employed you need all your wits about you. Nor do the customers of a hair-dressing salon welcome the smell of stale gin. I've always been grateful that in this respect at least she was temperate. She used drink; it didn't use her. So there were no money problems either. There was only the one problem as I sat down in the sitting-room with a pot of tea and put *Mood Indigo* on the record player. The problem was that I was growing excited again, that I could once again feel the soft hand on my penis, see Lorraine's lips drawn back over her teeth, feel the fullness of her breasts beneath my hand, settle down with *Mood Indigo* –

And then there'd be the other pictures – Audrey astride Jeff, her skirts around her waist, Jeff gasping, the smells of love, leather, petrol, and then the picture I hadn't to look at, the picture that took only a split second, the stocking-top and white flesh above it, the itch, the secret shameful itch, the muddy bank of the pool, the hands scrabbling, death tasting of mud and dog-dirt and vomit, dirty water filling the lungs, thick mud crammed down the throat, legs apart on the bed of the spare room, the smell of Burmese cheroots, the amusement in the words *Christ, I nearly came* – the shared secret, the dirty secret, the white rotten flesh, the spurt of my semen, the smell of Lorraine's face-powder – and my erection grew, I could see the shape of it under my trousers, and death grew and I came out in a cold sweat and suddenly there was no erection and I hated my body and hated myself for being a man. But I wasn't a man. Jeff with his solid six inches at any time was a man. I was a male impersonator, a freak.

What surprises me now is that I survived all this. That was how I felt in that deadly quiet house, the scene of all the action, every inch saturated with memories. Is it only self-pity when I say that there was no one to help me? No, because there wasn't. I never talked about it with my mother, because that would have made it even worse. My mother, with the exception of Sheila, is the most self-centred and selfish person I have ever known. She has never been any different. She isn't interested in anyone else's problems. She doesn't want to help anyone, unless by so doing she can help herself. I don't believe that she ever has had even a momentary pang of guilt about my father's death. The one and almost the only thing which she's been willing to do for me is to look after my material comforts. She has an easy-going disposition, she enjoys her work and she enjoys her leisure, and she doesn't want to disrupt the smooth and agreeable surface of her existence by the consideration of anything disagreeable. The one thing which would have made her lose her temper was for me to ask her for any help other than financial help. She didn't like talking about my father in any case. I suppose that somewhere beneath all those layers of selfishness might have existed a rudimentary conscience. But to have talked with her about sex would have made my flesh crawl.

There was the doctor, an oldish Scotsman with a sour disposition, whose chief interests were whisky and fishing. He was a staunch Presbyterian and considered psychiatry to be filthy nonsense. But he considered sexual problems to be filthy nonsense too. If I'd gone to him he'd probably have recommended Epsom Salts, a daily cold bath, and twenty-mile walks. He wasn't in the least like the lovable, unshockable, infinitely understanding doctors in TV series.

I'd only been to our local Methodist chapel twice – when I was christened, and for my father's funeral – but the minister, a bachelor in his middle thirties, wouldn't have helped me either. Jeff's parents were staunch Methodists, and Jeff said that the minister was very keen on youth, and you knew what that meant. He was broadminded and progressive and no doubt would have been delighted to have discussed my hang-ups with me; but I had a shrewd notion, based on what Jeff had told me and what little I'd seen of him head-patting and shoulder-squeezing, moist-eyed among the dear lads, that his advice would have boiled down to steering clear of women and forming healthy comradely relationships with older chaps, chaps who really *understood*.

It would of course have been possible for me to go to a psychiatrist in Manchester, and my mother, to be absolutely fair, would have paid for it as long as I didn't bother her with my reasons for needing one. The doctor wouldn't have been at all enthusiastic about sending me to one, but he would have if pressed. But, although I didn't have very much sense at twenty, I instinctively knew that once you've been to a psychiatrist it's a black mark against you. I've found out since that I was dead right. All other things being equal, when you're choosing someone for a job, you choose the chap who hasn't ever needed a head-shrinker. And insurance companies are very awkward about anyone who's a little dotty. This is very sad and unjust, but that's how the world is.

There were of course chaplains at the university, but they were all horrible. And the staff wasn't dedicated, to say the least of it. Their chief aim in life, as far as I could see, was to do as little work as possible themselves whilst making us do the maximum. I daresay that they'd have helped me with any problems connected with my work, but that was as far as it went. The most likely response from the few amongst them who bore any faint resemblance to human beings would be that if anyone needed any help with sex problems it was they themselves.

In short, at that place and that time what was bothering me was like cancer or losing a limb in an accident. There was nothing to be done. There was nothing to be done about *any* problem unless you were exceptionally tough or lucky or both. When I realised that I was damaged – being young I tried hard to believe that it would pass, but I knew very well that it wouldn't – I resolved at least to be successful in other ways. I knew that I could not depend upon having what other men had as far as sex was concerned; but, though I was no academic in the making, was never going to be a brilliant thinker, I knew that I had a quick mind, a retentive memory, and the ability to work hard. I too, you might say, could have a ten-inch prick. And when I'd finished my cup of tea I opened *The Managerial Revolution*, which wasn't properly speaking one of our set books, but which had been recommended to me as background reading. It's the books which you read outside the set books which make the difference between Honours and a Pass.

I'm still trying to avoid it. I'm closing my mouth. I'm being a big baby. I don't want the probe to go any further. And yet that's wrong. It isn't like that. It's like an operation at the Battle of Trafalgar, big wooden splinters have gone deep into my flesh and there's no anaesthetic except rum, and the loblolly men are holding me down and I'm screaming in agony and the splinters near the skin are out, there's blood all over the surgeon's hands and his operating apron is stiff with it and his face is running with sweat and his breath stinks of rum and the sharp point is reaching down for the deepest splinter, the point is a burning needle searching out every nerve and it's a cold and heavy weight, heavier than the ship, heavier than the sea, heavier than the whole world, pressing me down –

Quickly, now. The second stage. In the sitting-room of our house, the blinds drawn one November afternoon. Unbuttoning Lorraine's blouse. The small mother-of-pearl buttons. The blouse off, the bra off, the slip down to the waist. She won't allow me any more, but I feel, exultantly, that that is enough, almost too much. My mother will be home at six. But Lorraine, when, at three-thirty, I try to unfasten her skirt at the waist, says, 'Someone may come in.'

It is necessary, ridiculous though it may seem now, to remember it all. The third stage. It is dark at four o'clock, with the only light in the room the gas-fire. A heap of pink satin cushions on the floor. She has a dress which buttons down to the waist, reddish-brown in nylon jersey. The dress stays on her shoulders but her skirt is riding up.

She puts my hand under her skirt. She won't let me pull up the skirt; it's as if she doesn't object to anything as long as it can't be seen. Approaching the sound of the guns: the double-knit stocking-top after the smoothness below, the soft bare flesh, the incredible reality, learning fast, astonished by the size of it, the thick hair, the *convexity*, the airbrushed smoothness of the *Health and Efficiency* photos instantly contradicted; her hand reaching towards my groin, caressing outside, the practised un-buttoning. This is enough, too, and more than enough. And it was. I still feel that. *Any* physical intimacy with a woman is a superb experience. Their bodies are as if of a superior species, so soft and so strong, alive all the way through and all over; their sexuality isn't just between their legs, but diffused, and I don't mean only their breasts. And the phrases one uses to describe what I did to Lorraine are all ugly, nowhere near the truth. There was terror there too. The quality of being was different that dark November afternoon. It always had been different, but on that afternoon, touching the mystery, the origin of all mystery, there was a sense of time being worth more, of what one had thought of as being rolled gold changing to real gold, gold all the way through; and everything in the room was not simply what one saw and smelled and touched, but all its raw materials, thousands of skills, time compressed into the carpet, the curtains, the gas-fire, the furniture, sun and rain and the seasons in the tea on the table; and she had chosen her clothes, chosen the woollen dress and the white bra and the white nylon slip and the white knickers and the white suspender belt and the mid-tan stockings and the brown suède court shoes – there was more time stored in those, as if time were part of their molecular structure. You could never say that they were ordinary or dull, you could never say anything was ordinary or dull, or that my hands would ever be other than happy again, that they would ever forget their travels. I was both right and wrong: right to value properly what she gave me, right not to confuse it with wanting to spend the rest of my life with her, but wrong to concentrate so much upon my own pleasure, not to perceive that, when she gave, most of her pleasure was in giving pleasure, that when she took hold of me all of her pleasure was in giving pleasure. And I was wrong in a deeper, more damaging way because there was another person there, an unshaven beer-swilling slob, a manly man, a real man, one of the boys with hair on his chest, not only with plenty downstairs – a full six inches now – but plenty upstairs, a master of sexual technique, a real Casanova, a chap who knew what women liked, getting her well and truly warmed up, ready for it.

Ready for it. Ready for the big event. Ready to lose my cherry. Ready to be a winner, to prove myself. For every time I made love with Lorraine that third person was there, the tough, the hearty, the lout, the hooligan, the slob. Jeff had got ahead of me and I had to catch up with him. And I couldn't see, being only twenty and pig-ignorant, that it didn't matter a damn about catching up with Jeff, that it didn't matter a damn what he or anyone else thought of me, that in sex all that matters is what satisfies you and one other person. I would have been quite happy, I know now, to go on as we were going on, for us to *learn* about each other, to let what was going to happen happen, not to worry and not to hurry.

And now there is another double double whisky in front of me and I can't remember having poured it. *Not to worry and not to hurry*: that's what Sheila said to me a long time

ago. It would have been better if Lorraine had said it;
but how could she have learned it, having been brought up
where she was brought up? It would have been better,
too, if I'd loved her, or at least believed that I loved her.
But I had a horror of marriage at that time: it seemed to
me to boil down to being hurt. My excuse was that I
didn't want the distraction of a fiancée and marriage plans;
he rides the fastest who rides alone and all the rest of it.
Untrue, untrue, and here I am now staring at the parquet
flooring, sitting in this quiet room on Sugar Hill, sipping
whisky to keep images from my mind. Images? One
image: she is on her back in a clearing, bushes and trees
rustling in the wind, a car-rug underneath her, her legs
wide open. Or is she reclining on a reclining seat? Or is
she naked in a motel room or the bedroom of a company
flat? *Let's face it, Jim, one man's not enough for me . . . I'm a
good girl for just so long, then I grow restless . . . Ask no questions
and you'll be told no lies. And I won't ask you any questions, if
you see what I mean and I'm sure you do.* It's all coming out
now, she's in the armchair by the fire, a glass of whisky
in her hand, her legs are bare and she's wearing a mini-
dress because she likes showing off her legs, and I'm looking
at her legs. I can't help being turned on, though I hate
myself for being turned on. *As far as sex is concerned, I'm
like a man. Once, twice, and its smashing. And then I get bored.
It's never as good as you think it's going to be . . . I suppose I'm
searching for the perfect fuck . . .* Then her voice takes on a
complaining note. *Why did you give me all this to drink . . .*

Then don't drink it, you stupid bitch. Is that what I said? I
know very well I said that.

You don't want a divorce, do you?

I shook my head. I couldn't say anything. The idea of
not seeing her again made me feel literally sick.

Because I'm very fond of you. You're the only man I've ever been fond of, apart from Cliff. It's absolutely clear now, every word. It didn't happen in the past, it is *happening, it is going on.* She is in that chair and all the time I'm looking at her legs and my prick is actually hurting.

I just like men. She moistens her lips. *I don't think I'm a nympho. I can do without them for a long time, if I'm that way out.*

You should have been a whore, I say.

She laughs. *I like to pick and choose, darling. And I'm very choosy. Wouldn't care to have a dose, either. Do you know you've got a hard-on?*

Her legs open and she has no pants on; and I push the memory away, I switch off my mind, I go over to the record player and put on *Cabaret,* putting it to my favourite first. 'Tomorrow Belongs To Us' . . . That is the song with which we end all public meetings in my *white,* my *shining* town, that is the song that promises me that one day I shall be perfectly happy, that there will be no more past, no more regrets, that Sheila won't go out in the evenings by herself again . . .

I lie down on the sofa, my hand covering my eyes. The erection has subsided. I listen to the music, but it's not enough to stop me thinking. Perhaps I ought to try to listen to serious music, *good* music, but unless there are words and a tune, or at least a tune, music is nothing but a meaningless noise to me. Lorraine was shocked by this; I always seemed to be shocking her.

'Don't you ever feel sorry for poor people?' she'd ask me, her voice positively shaking with emotion.

'I don't feel sorry for anyone,' I'd answer with complete sincerity. It wouldn't be quite true now; since having Gareth and Sharon I can't bear to think of any children suffering. I wouldn't *like* to see any adult suffering, but I can put up with it with complete equanimity. Lorraine used to go on a great deal about people in foreign

129

countries: blacks in the USA, starving Indians, and even aborigines in Australia. She tried to get me to join the university Labour group, but I wasn't having any. I didn't join the Conservative group either. She deplored this almost as much as she deplored me not joining her lot.

But when we were, to use an old-fashioned word, necking she didn't talk much, and when she did talk it wasn't about politics. After I had had my orgasm we lay quietly in each other's arms. I didn't ask her if she was satisfied; such a question would never have occurred to me. I was satisfied and presumed that she was; it wasn't so much selfishness on my part as sheer ignorance.

After a while she sat up, gave me a cigarette (everyone smoked then) and said in a low voice: 'We'll get into trouble soon if we don't watch out.'

'I'm too happy to care.' It was true: I never have been ashamed or depressed after love.

'Perhaps we should stop seeing each other quite so much.'

'I like seeing you.'

'Is that all?' She stood up, smoothing down her skirt. 'Is that all?' Her eyes were wet.

I wasn't so young and stupid that I couldn't fill in the words which she wanted to hear from me, but I wasn't going to tell her that I loved her and I wasn't going to ask her to marry me. I had in mind a succession of mistresses, I really fancied myself as a great lover, I congratulated myself for having got so far with her and gloated a little over the amount of sexual technique I'd accumulated. And that was all nonsense – there is no such thing as sexual technique; there is only that one simple admonition: never hurry, never worry.

I stood up. 'I ought to use something,' I said. 'Then we couldn't get into trouble.'

'Oh, you're *hopeless*!' she cried, and ran out of the room.

I could hear her weeping as she went up the stairs into the bathroom.

I took the lock on the front door off the sneck and washed my hands in the kitchen sink, rather puzzled. It doesn't seem possible now either that I should be puzzled or that I should not be distressed by a woman's tears; but in fact I was rather pleased with myself for having power over her. Great lovers treat 'em rough.

She'd put on fresh make-up before she came downstairs again, and there was no trace of the tears. But when we were drinking tea she was unusually quiet and she had a strained expression – as if her face were on the verge of twitching – which I had not seen before. For a moment I felt a sense of loss, but of what I didn't know.

Now the probe had nearly reached the splinter. A fortnight later, at the beginning of December. Snow on the ground: white on our estate, already black in the town. A gunmetal-grey sky. It doesn't matter what happened in between. There were lectures, the University Operatic and Dramatic Society did *Iolanthe*, the car got into a long frightening skid and I nearly knocked an old woman down (I can still see her gaping at me, apparently quite unable to move, like a hen with its beak on a chalk line). I went on a pub crawl of Manchester with Jeff and he told me that he was now, as he put it, getting it regular from Audrey, and I bought the *something* at a barber's in Manchester. I kept looking at it in the bathroom and the more I looked at it the more I doubted whether I did want to have sexual intercourse with Lorraine. The flesh-coloured rubber, the large ring, the talc it was powdered with, made sex an activity of machines, of robots actuated by motors and springs or, worse still, a *medical* activity, hygienic, sterilised.

Quickly, now. She wouldn't take all her clothes off; after a very short time she took off her knickers and pulled up her skirt, her legs wide apart, and lay there with her eyes closed. I took off my trousers, and shoes and socks, feeling faintly ridiculous, and got out the condom. There had been an erection until then; suddenly it was lost, suddenly I was no longer a man but a little boy – there was no desire. I did the worst thing which I could do, which was to panic, frantically to rub myself, trying to will my penis to recover itself. It wasn't any use: will-power, courage, toughness, good health, none of these has anything to do with sexual desire. You want to or you don't, just as you're hungry or not hungry.

What was the reason for it? It isn't important now; but what broke me down, what unstrung the taut bow, was that this was the first time I'd really seen a cunt; I'd explored it with my hands, I'd got rid of some of my more naive misconceptions, but I hadn't *seen* it, hadn't realised how *stark* the female organ is, how stark and how complex; I still had a vision of it as a plain slit, a hole. For the first time I believed in a baby's head popping out from it, understood – and was shocked by – the attendant mess. What she had between her legs was blood and suffering, death and darkness and the hands scrabbling the muddy bank of the pool, the screaming, the contorted face going down in the dark dirty water. I was right to lie down beside her but I was wrong to think only of myself; I should have kissed her, told her that I loved her, talked gently to her, then gently, gently, slowly, slowly, have explored her, got to know her. I should have cared only about giving her pleasure; I shouldn't have thought about myself at all. But of course I only thought about myself; worse still, I had in my head a picture of myself telling Jeff about it, being one of the club, losing my ring, being a real man, and in the process, of course, turning Lorraine into a non-person.

'Hurry,' she said, her eyes still closed. 'What's the matter?' Her hand reached for me. 'Where's it gone? Where's it gone?' Her hand felt cold; it had never felt cold before. And nothing happened; I knew now that nothing would, and I stood up and put on my trousers. I felt better now in a strange way, my secret hidden.

She opened her eyes. 'What is the matter, Jim?'

'I thought I heard someone at the door,' I mumbled.

'There's no one at the door.' She sat up and put her knickers on and smoothed down her skirt. 'You don't love –' she gulped and her eyes moistened '– don't want me any more.' She stood up. 'I'll make some tea.'

I put on my socks and shoes, sat down, and lit a cigarette. I felt nothing. I wanted nothing. I looked forward to nothing. There wasn't any shame, any sense of failure; sentence had been passed, and there was nothing to be done about it.

I didn't go out with her again; when I saw her around the university, I said hello, and hello was all. I didn't take any girls out for two or three months, and when I did start again I didn't do any more than kiss them goodnight and I never went out with any of them more than twice. As they say, I kept it cool.

A week later I went with Jeff to the Seven Bells. It wasn't very enjoyable until the third pint; I hated all the men and was frightened of all the women. I couldn't help looking at them, but I knew now that it was no use. The strange thing was that the day after I'd failed with Lorraine I'd gone to bed with a copy of a pornographic magazine and had complete and successful intercourse with a rather wholesome-looking blonde named Vicki. Vicki spent A Day in The Country and what did it for me was a picture of her lying down amongst the hay, her skirt up to her stocking-tops and showing the edge of her knickers. Actually the magazine wasn't pornographic; today it wouldn't even earn the appellation of soft porn. But it turned me on and that was all that I cared about. I didn't, God knows why, reason that if Vicki gave me an instant and long-lasting erection there wasn't much wrong with me; and, as I've said, there was no one to help me. And maybe I was right: the difference was the difference between shooting on the target range and shooting in actual combat. I knew about this from Uncle Sidney – though I suspect that he never shot at anyone in combat but just kept on running.

That night at the Seven Bells, Jeff asked me about Lorraine. He was rather specific: he asked me if I'd put it in yet.

'I haven't bothered,' I said. 'Actually, I think she's gone off me.'

'A shame,' he said. 'In my opinion she'd be all the better for six inches of good stiff prick.'

'She's too bloody earnest for me. Gets on my tit ends, all that guff about the suffering worker.'

'It would mine a bit. I like to do all the talking; women are so damned sentimental. Is there anything here you fancy?'

I made some excuse about that too; I think that he was rather relieved since, though he wasn't badly off, picking up women in the Cocktail Bar at the Seven Bells was liable to be rather expensive. The girls at the university only expected to be paid for when you specifically said that you were flush. It's not very often that I look back at my time at the university, but when I do I have a sort of composite picture of the girls I took out there: sturdy, with fresh fair skin, rather serious, with grey flannel skirt and polo-necked sweater and clean well-brushed hair. Tennis and dances and picnics, long evenings of argument in the Union, the occasional star speaker from the great world outside; and these nice clean decent girls who mostly went to the university as virgins and graduated as virgins, despite the loudly proclaimed belief of some of them in free love. I had begun to bury the memory of what had happened – or rather what had not happened – with Lorraine, and by the time I graduated there was only a twinge from time to time. There wasn't so much pressure on the young as there is now; girls expected young men to try to go the full way, and the young men tried, but they weren't surprised when they weren't allowed to. So I wasn't all broken up by my failure, I always hoped that it would right itself. I couldn't believe that it was permanent. I suppose that this is the kind of moronic optimism which has kept the human race going for so long.

What fixed me was Louise, who was a supervisor at a branch of the chain store in Manchester where I went as a trainee executive after graduation. The store specialised in clothing and was both enlightened and profitable. Maybe they were a bit too enlightened; to me they always seemed to care more about the staff than the customer. It worked out very well in one way, because they kept their staff; but I always thought that their staff were lacking in charm, to say the least of it. You went there because the goods were cheap and sound; you didn't go there to give yourself a little lift, to be made a fuss of. I've always felt – and it's one of my few commendable characteristics – that most people lead pretty dreary lives and many lead pretty wretched lives, and that when they go to a stores they're entitled to a little bit of escape, a little bit of colour, a little bit of showmanship, a little bit of luxury. The stores in Manchester weren't tatty, they were scrupulously clean, they offered real value for money, they exchanged goods without question, but they were somehow bleak.

I went there shortly after graduation as a trainee executive. I learned a lot there, but I always knew that I wasn't going to stop there the rest of my life. It was a solid family business and there was no way of getting into the family. There is a Northern Nonconformist aristocracy, founded in the days of the penal laws against Nonconformism, and whatever it takes to become a member of that aristocracy I hadn't got. On the few occasions I met the men at the top, I liked them well enough, particularly the Chairman, old Josiah. I had an hour with old Josiah once – I'd been there three years and had managed to get a report through to him on the use and training of graduates in the business – and I think that he liked me.

He was a tall man – four inches over six foot – and always wore the same navy-blue serge suit with a stiff white collar and blue and white polka-dot tie and black boots and a gold pocket-watch with a heavy gold chain. He smoked a very old pipe which had been repaired with wire; but his tobacco was always Balkan Sobranie with a heavy admixture of Turkish. He had the kind of face which they don't make any more, with grey bushy eyebrows and a mane of grey hair, a Roman nose, and an air of being held together, like his body, by sheer strength of will. He would have been in his late sixties then. They say that thousands of brain cells die every day after you grow up, leading to senility, but all old Josiah's brain cells seemed to be there.

He sat there in his dark oak-panelled office, surrounded

by pictures of members of the family since the eighteenth century, firing questions at me which all added up to the fact that not only had he read and understood the report but that he had a shrewd idea of what was in my mind when I wrote it. I wasn't nervous or in the least frightened, but I was all keyed up. I had thought it best not to smoke since he hadn't specifically given me permission, and my mind was a shade too clear, everything was a shade too real. Smoking takes the edge off things.

He tapped the report with his pipe and then pushed across a silver box and opened it to reveal a few Churchman's Number One. 'Some good clear thinking here, young man,' he said.

I lit a cigarette. It had been in the box too long, but I enjoyed it.

'Thank you, sir. I think I've covered everything.'

'You're of the opinion that, at your university in particular, there's rather too much emphasis on the virtues of collectivism. You do realise that this family has a tradition of liberalism?'

I smiled. 'And of profits, sir.'

'Of profits and of staff welfare. They go together like bacon and eggs.'

'If you don't have the profits you won't have any staff welfare.'

'We'll talk again. In the meantime the Board will consider your report. It's just what we need. Mr Jesse will be *most* interested.' He held out his hand. 'I'll be watching you, Jim.'

And he would have watched me, and if I'd kept my nose clean and worked hard I would have been given promotion, ended up with a personal secretary and an office of my own and a cost-of-living-indexed pension, and all the many benefits of their little welfare state. But the real decisions would have been taken and the real money earned by members of the family like Mr Jesse, his eldest son. And that was why I left three years later.

That is what I told Cliff Droylsden. That is what I told Sheila. That is what I told everybody. I've almost begun to believe it myself. It did have something to do with it. And I fancied a change. But the main reason for my leaving Manchester was five foot one, slim, dark with brown eyes, a war widow eight years older than me, and was named Louise. She was the secretary of the Personnel Controller and I first met her when I was compiling the report for old Josiah. She was very helpful; she was one of the people, to be found in every large organisation, who knew the best person to go to – who isn't always the person to whom one's officially supposed to go.

It was quite a long time before I actually asked her to go out with me; I was going out with other girls – on the same basis as at the university – and I expect that she rather frightened me. She obviously liked me, and quite obviously was experienced. I somehow felt that she wouldn't be contented with kisses or with heavy petting. And she had a twelve-year old son, which wasn't exactly a recommendation. On the other hand – and I think that this thought was never very far from me – an older woman was exactly what men in my position were supposed to need. And I had by then a small flat in Wilmslow, near Dickinson Road – I had grown tired of commuting and I expect my mother didn't want a grown-up son around – so there was an operation theatre available. And that was the trouble. I viewed her not as a woman but as a physician. She would cure me, she would make me a man. And that isn't any use. That isn't what sex is all about. I don't say that some men can't use sex – but I wasn't one of them.

Get this over with quickly too. The headquarters near the Piccadilly Station, a blackened old Victorian building long since demolished. I've been working late, and I leave through the Personnel Office, where Louise is just putting the cover on her typewriter. It's November and it's raining, but not very hard. It must have been a Thursday night; in my recollection the atmosphere was *Thursday* – not much money around, but anticipation in the air, subdued but cheerful. Dealing as I do with the public, you have a different picture of each day of the week; if you haven't, you'd better leave the retailing business.

I'd merely passed the time of day with Louise before, but there wasn't much alternative, there being people all around us. That evening I came right out with it.

'Would you care for a drink, my dear?' I put on a mock seducer's voice.

She hesitated, then smiled.

'Just lead me to it,' she said. 'I've had the hell of a day.' She had a white frilled blouse and a black skirt and tan stockings; she looked tired, with faint smudges under her eyes, but that somehow seemed to make her look younger, more approachable. I kissed her lightly on the mouth; she recoiled slightly with surprise, then returned the kiss open-mouthed and moistly. I felt the beginnings of an erection. That's good to remember and I needn't touch my whisky. That can't be taken away from me and that can't be spoiled: the taste of her lipstick and her tongue, the pressure of her small breasts and her surprisingly full belly. And the rain outside and the swish of motor tyres and the lights of the city. I've often wished I didn't like women so much – I'd be a millionaire if I didn't like them, and no doubt a happier man – but who or what else can give us such moments?

That was the best of it. It was good coming out into the street, the rain on our faces, and the first drink was good. It had been the hell of a day for me too, and I had gin and tonic along with her in the bar at the Midland. I never drank during the day – I very rarely do now – and I needed and deserved the drink. I very rarely drink gin but there are certain moods when it hits the spot immediately, gives you a quick lift, makes you feel that the world is a good place – and with gin and tonic, unlike whisky, there doesn't have to be any nonsense about savouring its taste. It isn't supposed to do you good either. You drink it for a quick lift or to get pissed out of your mind, and that night I'd been seriously thinking of the latter; I did have some friends in Manchester but none were available that night, and I felt rather lonely.

I'm doing it again, I'm picking out what was good about the evening, I'm evading the point. And the point was not sitting in the Midland relaxing with her, nor having dinner there – smoked salmon, chicken *vol-au-vent*, cheese and fruit, a bottle of hock – but what happened in my flat. There was her naked body, and my shock of delight. Her body seemed fuller and softer naked; I should have taken my time, I should have soothed her, I should have quietened her down a little, I should have told her that what should grow would grow, I should not have panicked, I should not have been in such a hurry. That is enough. What should have grown did grow in her hand; but what should have happened much later happened almost immediately – a spasm, a sneeze, a strangled ecstasy.

'Don't worry,' she said, putting on her clothes. 'It

could happen to anyone. You've had a bit too much to drink, that's all.'

But it wasn't the drink. It was me. With no excuse, with a place of my own. With all the time in the world, with an experienced woman. I knew, as I dressed, that she had written me off. There would be no repeat performance. She wanted a man, a real man. The want of it would be facing her the morning after. And facing the other women in her office. I don't think that this should have bothered me; in the Fifties women kept their mouths shut about such things. But I already imagined a circle of giggling women, gloating over my failure, already saw myself as a sort of eunuch Corn King, torn apart by scornful Maenads.

That night I drank half a bottle of whisky, then fell asleep with my clothes on. The next night I went to the pictures by myself, and then when I returned to the flat I cried myself to sleep.

That's it. That's everything. The splinter is out. The pain is over. The surgeon wipes the sweat from his face and has another mouthful of rum. The loblolly boys let me go.

There are always compensations. I looked at the other people at HQ and realised that though they did their jobs well enough, they weren't really committed, particularly the university types. And I realised my vocation, which was quite simply to be a good shopkeeper. The others had all sorts of interests; their jobs bought them the leisure for these interests. Some of them even wanted to change society. I wanted to understand it. I wanted to understand what made people go into some shops rather than into others, I wanted to understand what made people buy, and I wanted to understand not only what they bought but what they thought they were buying. I had the Hillman and I spent most of my spare time looking at every kind of shop, pricing all kinds of goods, examining every kind of customer. The more I went into it, the more I was convinced that I was in the wrong kind of retailing, that what I really was interested in was running a large department store, preferably one which had gone downhill, which would give me the chance to show how clever I was.

There's one piece of wisdom which I learned after the *débâcle* with Louise: your work never lets you down. You'll never be really lonely or defeated as long as you enjoy your work. I did enjoy my work when I was at Manchester and I learned a great deal: old Josiah wasn't scientific himself but he knew enough to employ people who were. Everything the stores sold passed all the tests, and the selling was planned down to the tiniest detail of layout, siting, lighting, and so on. And there were no passengers at HQ, though personally I always thought that they were a bit too fussy about staff welfare – in fact, altogether too high-minded for me. But I resisted the pressure to shunt me off into the Personnel Department and I put in a lot of time on the merchandising side, finding out what people in general and men in particular actually wore and what they would pay for it and what were the standards of decent clothing. It was good solid stuff and I wore a lot of it myself, though only when it was plain or couldn't be seen. There's no sense in paying a lot for plain-coloured socks or plain-coloured sweaters or swimming-trunks or underwear or white shirts; but, to choose only one ex-ample, I'd feel like throwing away a patterned shirt if I saw every Tom, Dick and Harry wearing it. I have a lot of theories about men's clothes, most of which I've put into practice very profitably at Droylsden's; and it was after that episode with Louise that I started really thinking about my job. And not only about men's clothes, but just about everything that is sold at a department store. I even started reading purposefully – about the history of clothes, pottery, ornaments, jewellery, furniture, and so on.

I found that there was a Young Conservative branch in the town – the Conservative party had bucked up towards the end of 1948 – and found it the answer to at least one of my problems, which was loneliness. Jeff had taken a job teaching in Derbyshire, and the people I'd gone to the university with had scattered all over the place, and the people I'd gone to the grammar school with I'd grown away from. Aunt Ada had died when I was sixteen, and she was my only relation in the town; what it boils down to was that I wasn't a member of any group in the town. There was only the Young Conservatives; I was never very interested in the political side of it, but I enjoyed the social side. I took out girls from time to time but never more than once, and at the Conservative Club there was always someone to have a drink with. My sex life was confined to girls like Vicki until I discovered through someone I met at the Conservative Club the existence of real pornography, the hard stuff. In one way the recollection is rather pathetic: a clean-cut healthy young man sitting up in bed staring at black-and-white photos of naked women, mostly slim and dark-haired, some middle-aged, but some, contrary to the common misconception, positively beautiful. It was rather sad, and it was a rather sad flat on the top floor of a Victorian terrace house – a sitting-room with dark brown fitted carpet, pale yellow flowered wallpaper, piebald blue velvet curtains, and the minimum of dark, battered second-hand furniture, a bedroom with a brass-railed double bed and white distempered walls, a tiny kitchen and a tiny bathroom. That's all I remember, except that there was black and green linoleum on the bedroom floor and the effect was of spreading mildew. It was sad but it was warm, with huge old-fashioned radiators which snorted and clanked all the night through and two battered but efficient gas-fires, one in the bedroom and one in the sitting-room. My mother, who with all her faults was never mean, paid the rent and would gladly have paid more for something better, or even have furnished and decorated a flat for me, but I was beginning to be tired of the North. Nor, despite the episode with Louise, did I want to settle down to being a house-proud bachelor. I didn't really see how I ever could get married, I didn't really want to get married for a while, but I wasn't prepared to reconcile myself to being a bachelor all my life. I wasn't ever going to try with a woman again, but somehow I couldn't accept the fact of impotence; it didn't make any sense when I looked at those girls, naked except for black nylons, their legs apart, and felt my penis rise without my even touching it.

It was bad enough then, but it could be worse now. Most girls then didn't really expect to be poked unless they'd known the man for quite a while and unless he was serious about them. There wasn't so much stimulation about; it wasn't presumed that a man is always in a state of randiness. People didn't go on about it all the time. Even show-business people didn't tell all at the drop of a hat. There weren't any sex shops and the nudes in live shows had sequins or sticking plaster at the three crucial areas and stayed immobile. In nudist films – which was virtually the only kind of film in which one saw the naked female body – there was always a patch of deep shadow or a beach-ball or a newspaper or a hand concealing the genitals.

It was a strange period in my life. I don't like to think of it very much now. There was so much of it which was spent by myself that the week-ends at home became more and more important to me. My mother wasn't much company; she was at the salon all day on Saturday, and when she came home it was only to change and generally tart herself up for an evening out; and she wouldn't generally return until the small hours. Sometimes she wouldn't return until about ten in the morning; though she always 'phoned me, generally from a pub, with a hubbub of voices and music in the background.

We didn't talk very much when we were alone together and I never inquired into her private life. In fact, I chose not to think about it. I was in a big enough mess as it was. Day and night I carried with me the consciousness of failure, of not being a man, of being different from the rest; what frightened me was that there were times when I hated all other men, even old men. They were having or had had what I longed for above anything else, they took it for granted, they said that they'd rather have a good dinner, they envied me for being a bachelor with a nice little car and a place of my own and no worries. I would have given up everything I had to have changed places with any of them, mortgage and squalling babies and nagging wife and all. I would find myself appalled by the bitter envy which would devour me whenever I saw any man and woman together, and particularly the young. Even routine announcements of local weddings in the newspapers would be as if specially printed to hurt me.

God knows what lies ahead of me. I've reached the age now when I definitely know I'm not going to live for ever. I've had enough experience of life to know that a man's life may be going swimmingly and then illness or accident strikes; one moment the sun is shining and you're floating on your back half asleep and half gloriously alive, and then it's agony and blackness as the shark drags you down – but whatever happens I don't have to live through that period again.

The worst of it was that it had to be secret. There would have been no sympathy from anyone if I'd told them. It's the one misfortune which no one pities. It's shameful, it's embarrassing, it's unclean, it's comic, it's worse even than physical cowardice. And I had the extra shame, the badge of apparent physical deficiency, I was a freak, I had another secret to hide. To this day I can't make water in the kind of urinal which doesn't have compartments, but have to go into the WC and lock the door.

That's enough for now. I've come through on the other side. I've survived. I've kept my secret, even from Sheila. I've kept out of the hands of the psychiatrists, I've not asked anyone for pity or for understanding, no one has helped me. Or if they did, it was without knowing it, it was for their own benefit, they thought that they were taking something from me, they didn't know that I was taking something from them. Only in my *white* town, my *shining* town, do people tell the truth to each other, do people actually *want* to help each other, and even there it's pretty well understood that it would be on a basis of you scratch my back and I'll scratch yours. I don't think that anyone with the disability which I had then would be allowed into my town – we'd smell the septic wound, be offended by the weakness.

The only exception I've ever known to the rule was Henry. He did help me when he advised me – or rather my mother – that I should get a degree. Henry was also the only exception I've ever known to my mother's rule of not having a man stay the night whilst I was in the house. That must have been about 1963; I'd been in Manchester nearly five years.

I'd come home about half-past ten after a rather dreary evening pub-crawling with Jeff, who was on the point of becoming engaged to Audrey – of all people – who'd turned up in his life again, having got a job in the same town. It was dreary because he'd told me in some detail about his other sexual involvements and his renewal of the sexual involvement with Audrey, and I'd been forced to keep up with him to some extent and naturally had been forced to lie. This had depressed me, and he was depressed to begin with because he was both keen on Audrey and not keen on marriage. I was depressed because of my envy and depressed because I could see the stage approaching when all my age-group were married. We were supposed to be well into the Swinging Sixties by then, but the news hadn't yet reached my home-town. Once you married – particularly among the middle classes – that was the end to nights out with the boys, and indeed to all your bachelor social life. I had the feeling of change, a sort of cyclic irresistible change which was leaving me behind – Jeff was as it were about to fly south for the winter leaving me behind with my broken wings.

My mother came in with Henry at about eleven when I was drinking a cup of tea by the gas-fire. It must have been winter; it was very cold. Henry was rather drunk, staggering and mumbling. He was a large man with a round rather flat-featured face and small bright black eyes, who on the few occasions I met him was dressed rather loudly, more like a bookie than a solicitor. That night he had a camel-hair overcoat, a reddish-brown and gold check suit, a gold silk shirt, a bright red and gold silk tie, and reddish-brown suede shoes. He had grey hair, short by modern standards, but long by the standards of Northern professional men; it was normally brushed smoothly back but that evening it was dishevelled. I took off his coat – I was surprised by its lightness – and helped him up the stairs to the bathroom.

He appeared again in a very short time, smelling of Pear's soap and Canoe cologne and with his hair brushed smoothly again. 'It's all right, my boy,' he said, 'I am suffering from no discomfort. Your mama is over apprehensive. I shall *not* require your assistance down the stairs.'

'Just as you like, sir,' I said to him, but kept an eye on him nevertheless; he was steadier than when he'd gone up the stairs and now, miraculously, fully coherent.

I led him into the sitting-room and steered him into a chair by the fire, opposite mine. He sat down with a sigh of relief.

'Home,' he said. He blew a kiss at my mother. 'Though indeed, my dear, home is wherever you are.'

'I'll make up a bed for you,' she said. 'You're not driving any farther tonight.'

'It will be necessary to inform my beloved wife,' he said. He had a deep voice with the kind of accent which uneducated people mean when they use the term *educated* – beautifully enunciated, very precise, a sort of aural copperplate.

'Your beloved wife is in London,' my mother said. 'But the housekeeper has already been informed.' She frowned at him. 'I don't think you should have any more of the hard stuff. Why don't you have a nice cup of tea?'

'I am sixty years old, my dear Valerie, and I know what I need. I'm going to ask Jim to give me a large whisky, in which I hope he will join me.'

'Just as you like,' my mother said. She stifled a yawn. 'I'll put a hot-water bottle in your bed. Jim will get you whatever you need. I'm tired out. Good-night.'

'Good-night, my dear,' Henry said.

'Good-night,' I said. At that moment I rather admired my mother, and I could see her attraction for Henry. She never nagged and she never fussed and she never made herself a martyr. If she was tired, she went to bed; if Henry wanted whisky on top of a skinful, she let him have it.

'A most perspicacious woman,' he said after she had gone. 'I've been rather obnoxious this evening, I'm afraid. Feeling sorry for myself. I passed my sixth decade this week.'

'I wouldn't have thought it, sir.'

'Call me Henry. You see, Jim, I have two worlds. There's the professional world – very discreet, very respectable, very temperate. I have various business interests too. I must be a positive monument of rectitude. And there is another world, where one *unbuttons*. Where one relaxes completely . . . Do you follow me?'

'I follow you perfectly, Henry.' I wasn't very happy at being able to follow him perfectly; an angry sickness possessed me for a moment.

'Drunk though I am, Jim, I'm sensitive to shades of voice and even the most fleeting expression. You'd be surprised how often relaxation means for me simply that no demands will be made, either emotional or financial. As far as I'm concerned, do you know what your mother's most endearing quality is? *She doesn't give a damn.*'

'That's true enough, Henry,' I said, rather bitterly. 'You've put your finger on it there.'

'My wife and I, you know, have an agreement. We keep out of each other's way. It isn't the same thing. My wife meddles with other people; she tries to dominate them. Your mother doesn't.' He sipped his whisky with enjoyment. 'Don't try to change people, Jim. Not even in business. Find out what they're like and proceed on that basis.' He paused, took the rest of his whisky at one gulp, and held out his glass. 'I don't do this very often,' he said. 'Do you know, Jim, I enjoyed knocking that Scotch back? You're supposed to *sip* it, you see . . . So I said, to hell with it. Thumbing my nose at the conventions . . . I've got everything I want, don't you see? Have *you* got everything you want?'

'Far from it,' I said.

'I don't think that you'll get much more here. What little meat is left on the carcass in Lancashire, people like me have grabbed up.' He yawned. 'I've been an awkward devil tonight. Sending food back, complaining about the wine – I felt *that way out*, as they say . . . It isn't here, you know, Jim.' He was looking at me with an almost terrible concentration. '*It isn't here.*'

I was startled by his tone. 'What isn't here, Henry?'

'Whatever it is that you're so desperately looking for. You have to go away to find it.' He sipped his whisky. 'I went to boarding-school and I went to Oxford and I went to the Middle East but I've never really got away. So I never have been contented.'

'Perhaps you never would have been.'

'I was going to sit up all night drinking. But I'm too damned old . . .' It was as if he hadn't heard me. 'Your mother's talked with me about you.'

'I can manage without her help. Or yours.' I was beginning to feel really bitter.

He held up a surprisingly small and white hand. 'Of course you can manage. You've done very well. But it's possible that you could do even better . . . I might be able to give you some advice . . .'

'I can manage to work out my future for myself.' I thought of my mother upstairs in her pink and white bedroom, from which long since all traces of my father had been removed. It was a boudoir, not a bedroom, with a pink padded satin headboard and white spindly furniture and a white 'phone extension under a crinoline doll; the bed was king-size with a Dunlopillo mattress, and I don't know how it got through the door. I thought of that bed and I thought of my mother's smooth face and her smooth hair, still black in middle age, and her smooth thighs and Henry's small white hands and I wanted to kill him, then kill her. I couldn't decide how to do it but I wanted to bloody that sleek grey hair and put out those bright black little eyes and leave him propped up at the wheel of the Rolls outside. It passed, so I never got round to deciding how I should kill my mother. But I didn't try very hard to keep the hatred out of my voice. He should not have been there. None of them should have been there.

He smiled, showing white strong teeth that weren't false. 'I don't blame you for not liking me.'

I took a deep breath. 'I didn't say that I didn't like you.'

'My dear boy, no one likes me very much. I'm too clever and too rich. And I'm always right. It's a wonder that I haven't been murdered long since.'

I had to laugh. 'It might happen sooner than you think,' I said.

He shrugged. 'My family has never made old bones.'

'My father didn't,' I said. 'He was just past thirty when he died.'

'That's sad. My son was twenty when *he* died, a long way from home. Which doesn't solve your problem. The solution to your problem is to go South. Have you ever thought of that?'

I was overwhelmed by a tremendous loneliness, worse than anything I'd ever experienced before. South: the word was not warm but cold. I had a picture of pine trees and snow, of empty streets with me walking them alone, of old age coming upon me like a speeded-up film, of a small room with bare walls and a hospital bed, of white coats and impersonal appraising stares, of huge offices and work I couldn't understand, of the walls around me dissolving to let in the chilly night air. Henry was power, Henry was the father figure, Henry was looking at me now and all I could do was shake my head.

And next year in the spring I was the men's-wear buyer at Droylsden's, with a small flat – a tiny bathroom, a kitchenette, a tiny bedroom, a small sitting-room – in the town, ten minutes' walk from the stores. Henry had looked around, Henry had seen people, Henry had no doubt promised favours in the future, for that is how things are done. I learned afterwards that some people on the selection board weren't too keen on me; Droylsden's had an up-market image and they were frightened that I'd downgrade it. And it's possible that the Merchandising Manager – the fool's dead now – thought that I might be all too efficient, might one day tidy up and fumigate his cosy scruffy little kingdom. But from the first moment I sensed that Clifford Droylsden, the Managing Director, and the Chairman, Simon Droylsden, were on my side. Clifford was about fifty then, a tall thin man in a rumpled suit with a lined, bony face and a Roman nose, and a clipped, nervous way of speaking. He was never still, always fiddling, his eyes darting from face to face and object to object as if seeking help in what he was about to say. Simon had the same Roman nose, but was altogether sleeker and fatter and more placid; I remember that he had a very light grey suit and a purple tie with matching handkerchief. I always hesitate before saying that a chap's in show business, but I knew that Simon was even before I heard him speak. I came to the conclusion that not only was he in show business but he wasn't really in the department store business. He was doing all that a Chairman should do, but his heart wasn't in it; somebody was pulling the strings, but who?

That was the first time I met Sheila. Simon's secretary was off sick, and she acted as secretary. I'd like to say that I knew immediately what she would mean to me, that it was love at first sight. But that day she was simply a dark-haired smooth-faced girl in her middle twenties, Clifford's very competent secretary, who knew where all the bodies were buried. I had in any case a feeling that she and Clifford had something going, in which I was of course dead right. It wasn't that they gave each other long smouldering glances or took the opportunity to touch each other whenever possible; it was that they were too formal, too correct, for boss and secretary. They just weren't friendly enough, they weren't warm enough, and he was a warm, friendly man. I liked him from the first and he liked me, and that is what business is all about. I don't now ever take on anyone whom I don't instinctively like, no matter what his qualifications are; if I don't like him I can't work with him, and neither can anyone else.

All this is important. The town itself is important, because I liked it from the start. It's a Surrey commuter town, some thirty miles from London, which has grown up with the railways; it has absolutely no architectural distinction, it grew up any how, people living in places like Guildford and Weybridge and Chertsey and even Woking look down their noses at it, but I like it because it's clean and

153

there are a lot of trees and, even though times are hard recently, it's a great deal more prosperous than my home town and, what is more, hasn't been redeveloped. Droylsden's has the prime site, with a huge multi-storey car-park virtually next-door, and prime site it will remain because the bottom's dropped out of redevelopment now and is likely to stay dropped.

When I returned to the hotel, some ten minutes' walk from Droylsden's, it was about six o'clock. It was a fine April evening and the bar looked a trifle tatty in the sunlight, but that didn't in the least diminish my euphoria. I ordered a pint of bitter and was just sitting down with it when Sheila and a large red-faced man came in.

'Hello there,' she said. 'Celebrating?'

'Of course. Won't you have one? And your friend?'

The friend grunted something I couldn't hear; he didn't seem terribly keen on joining me. But Sheila smiled and sat down beside me, and he sat down with her, glaring at me and drumming thick fingers on the table.

'This is Tom Slob,' she said. 'Tom Slob, Jim Seathwaite.' She smiled at me. 'I collect slobs. Some girls collect dolls, some collect jewellery, but I collect slobs.'

I thought it best to disregard this; Tom was bigger than me, and his embarrassment was visibly increasing. 'What would you like to drink?'

'A Bloody Mary. Tom will have a lager because he's driving.'

I gestured at the barman but he was already measuring out the vodka.

'He knows me,' Sheila said. 'Everybody knows me. Now, he isn't a slob.' The barman in fact was young and rather good-looking in a swarthy kind of way; I was surprised to discover that I resented her interest in him far more than I resented her interest in Tom. For a sexual interest there was: I could feel the tension between them.

'You're trying to stir things up,' Tom said. He didn't have a regional accent, but he didn't have a public-school accent either.

'*I* didn't want to come here,' she said.

'What's wrong with it?'

She grimaced. 'Brown and red and tarnished mirrors and plastic-topped tables. And shabby carpet.' She turned to me. 'Droylsden's would have paid the bill for a decent hotel, you know.'

'It was the only one I could get into here. I wanted to look round the stores.'

'You're very serious, aren't you? Why aren't you married?'

It was as if she knew all my secrets. 'I haven't met anybody who'll have me.'

'So you say. What do you think of our Chairman?' She giggled. 'I think he fancies you.'

Nothing can be more ridiculous than to proclaim one's sexual normality; you either are or you aren't. So I thought I would use her; the more information the better. 'I wondered who the real Chairman was.'

'Did you? You're not just a pretty face, are you?' She sipped her Bloody Mary. 'The real Chairman is Cliff's wife. She has the money.'

Tom guffawed. 'She doesn't have Cliff though, does she?'

I'm not so sure about that. Davina has always done exactly what she wanted to do. If she were to die tomorrow I'm sure that we'd discover that she'd so arranged things that she'd still be in charge. I sometimes suspect that she arranged things so that I met Sheila that evening. She's a very clever woman: she never pushes anyone too far, she never flourishes the big stick. Or at least she didn't then, because that was boom-time. If you pushed people too far, there was always somewhere else that they could go. The number of options has dropped sharply now for all of us.

I didn't meet her until two months later at the Summer Social. This was a Droylsden institution along with the Staff Dinner and Staff Dance in November and December. She would have been about forty then, small, plump and pretty, with enormous dark eyes. She had a low-cut white taffeta dress; the material was so light that the breeze across the lawn made it ripple. After a while you forgot the wheel-chair. But there were deep lines from nostril to mouth that her make-up could not hide.

I had a different picture of her that day from Sheila. 'She's an old bitch,' Sheila said. 'Had a car accident soon after she was married. Takes it out on everyone. Still fancies herself, though.'

I noticed that Sheila had a very faint line of dark down on her upper lip. It wasn't a moustache or anything like it; it was only because the sunlight was so strong that I could see it. I wanted to stroke it, very gently, scarcely touching it, sensing each tiny hair through my finger-tips. Strangely enough, that's the one thing she has never permitted. Her eyebrows, those dark perfect arches, her eyelids over the large dark brown nearly black eyes, her cheeks – so soft that they seem scarcely like flesh at all – her full lips, her smooth level forehead – all this can be caressed, very gently, doing homage with my hands. But not there, never there.

I'm puzzled that I felt no lust for her on that first meeting. (At the interview I had other things beside sex on my mind; she was merely a piece of boardroom furniture.)

Perhaps it was the rather severe clothes – the white linen shirt with the blue tie, the navy-blue skirt, the black court shoes. But the skirt was above her knees and she had black stockings and her legs were very good. I think that she frightened me. She seemed too aggressive, too experienced. I could imagine her rapping out orders to which I could not respond. And perhaps, as I say, I had other things on my mind besides sex. Although from my visit to Droylsden's I could see all sorts of inefficiency to be straightened out, I couldn't tell how to set about it, even in my own department of men's-wear. It was a long climb to the position where I could sort out the whole stores, and in the meantime there was a new buying policy to be worked out in men's-wear. The *quality* of their stock was first-rate, but even old Josiah would have perceived that it was ten years behind the times. All this was running through my head – in addition to the practical problem of finding a flat and adjusting myself to an entirely new way of life – whilst I was talking to Sheila, so it isn't surprising that I didn't receive whatever signals she was sending out.

She did send one out that I remembered on going to bed that night. It was just before she left.

'I collect mugs too,' she said to me as she rose from the table.

'You mean pots? They're very interesting.'

She punched me playfully in the ribs. 'No, mugs. The opposite of slobs. Decent trusting chaps. Softies.'

'Am I a mug?'

'I haven't made my mind up. See you around.'

I think that she had. She's always known which side her bread was buttered on. Mugs or slobs, she has used us all. I imagined for a long time that I chose her, but she chose me, just as my mother chose my father and Uncle Sidney and Henry and Rolf and all the others. And just as Davina chose me at the Summer Social at Cliff's house on St George's Hill. Why 'Summer Social', and not 'Garden Party'? It was, after all, a garden party for executive personnel and a few long-serving sales staff and general dogsbodies: but the term Summer Social had always been used. It was the occasion when Davina met new executives, kept in touch generally and, most important of all, showed everyone who was the boss. She was the boss, she was the real Chairman, because it was her money which had saved Cliff five years before my coming there.

I suppose that I should have been impressed by that huge white house with the six acres of grounds, the tennis court and swimming pool, the separate staff quarters; but it struck me as being ridiculously large for a childless couple. Cliff wants to sell it now and has been forced to come down to a hundred and fifty from two hundred; in the meantime it's eating up money and doing nothing for it. What I was interested in that day was who had the power. And it was Davina.

'So you're the barbarian from the North,' she greeted me with.

'You'll have to civilise me, Mrs Droylsden.' I took her hand; it was slim but surprisingly strong.

'Since you're nice-looking, call me Davina.' She smiled; it was an unexpectedly sexual smile. 'We mustn't civilise you too much or we'll rob you of your crude energy and drive . . . I hear that you've already been making changes . . . What's this about ties?'

As I looked at her full creamy breasts an erection was beginning. I wondered if she still slept with Cliff; if she did, wouldn't she need help? 'It's only a small matter, Davina.'

'Explain it to me nevertheless.'

'Some of the ties don't have labels, except a little one to give the country of origin and material. Men don't like ties without a brand label.'

'But no one sees it, surely?'

'It's a question of who buys it. The ties are there to be sold. Any brand name is OK, some more than others. But obviously if the manufacturer can't be bothered, the best thing to do is to put on a Droylsden's label. Then the buyer feels he's got something special.'

'You've thought a lot about it, obviously.'

'What's in my mind is a clean sweep and a summer sale and starting afresh. Everything's changing, we're miles behind.'

'Our customers are very conservative,' said Clifford, who'd been standing beside her smiling benignly, a consort rather than a king. 'We wouldn't want to be *too* trendy.'

'Even the middle-aged are loosening up,' I said. 'You didn't get that very nice bright blue jacket from our stock, did you?'

He smiled. 'Aquascutum, actually. They've got the choice –'

'Exactly, sir. And we should have the choice.'

'You must have a talk with Mr Hobbs,' Davina said. 'And so must you, Cliff.'

'I'll see to it,' he said, his eyes on Sheila, who was

talking to a young man in the far corner of the garden. 'Excuse me, my dear, I must see my secretary –'

'*Must* you?' Davina said, as he hurried off. '*Must* you?' She smiled at me. 'Have you got a girl, Jim?'

'Not at present, Mrs Droylsden.'

'Davina. I'm middle-aged, not moribund. Why haven't you got a girl?'

People kept asking me this; I decided that in future I would invent a fiancée in Lancashire.

'I hate to be tied down.'

'Why are you staring at my bosom?' There was no annoyance in her voice; she was simply requesting information.

'It's a very pretty bosom.'

She laughed. 'Fair enough. After all, I do my share of crotch-watching. Does that shock you? Or do you think cripples shouldn't have any sexual desires?'

'Now you're implying that I really am a barbarian, Davina.' By now I was becoming uncomfortable; she glanced downwards and I had a sudden picture of her taking me into the house, propelling her wheel-chair rapidly. Would there have to be help? Wouldn't that put me off? The picture dissolved and she patted my hand.

'We'll meet again soon, Jim, and have a long talk.' She turned to Simon Droylsden who was flouncing up to her in a cream-coloured silk suit.

Is she a friend? Yes, she is a friend. She always was a friend, from the first day that I met her. She could have been more than a friend but for overturning her Bugatti on the A4 soon after her marriage but, though intercourse was technically possible for her, in actual fact she'd resigned herself to doing without it long since. Her energies went into being the shadow Chairman of Droylsden's, which, as I discovered that day, didn't prevent her from still being interested in sex.

Sipping my whisky very slowly now, I'm grateful for Davina. She gave me what I needed in those four years before I married. She gives me what I need now: she is a woman friend with whom I don't have to – indeed cannot possibly – go to bed. We don't meet very often and when we do we mostly talk about business. But there is nothing we cannot talk about and one day I may tell her everything. I think of that now, I want before I die to tell one other human being what it has been like all these years, how much I have been hurt, how I have endured – and how, above all, they have helped me to endure. She told me once that I helped her too. That was a long time later, after Sharon was born. I was sitting by Davina's bed, the white hospital bed with all the cranks and pulleys and levers – more like an operating-table than a bed, incongruous in that large airy chintzy feminine room – massaging her neck and looking with pleasure at her still firm breasts.

'I couldn't have managed without you,' she said. 'I don't know how I did without you all those years. You still get a kick out of my breasts, don't you?'

'I always will, Davina.'

'I'm glad you do. They're all I've got left, I'm a terrible mess down below.' She unloosened her shoulder straps. 'Look at them whilst they're still worth looking at.'

'Oh. You know what it does, don't you?'

'I should know by now. Don't be nervous. Cliff never comes up when I'm with you. No one will. Not ever. Do you know that Noel Coward song? *If love were all – heigh-ho, if love were all* . . . Move closer, Jim. There now, I'll take it very slowly . . . That bastard Cliff only ever let me once. What harm does it do?'

'No harm – at all. Oh, Christ, Christ, merciful Christ!'

'I'll just stop and touch. Like a butterfly. I feel so close to you. What do you want? Tell me what you want.'

'Nothing now. Don't stop.'

'You want that rotten little whore. She's got you, she's got Cliff, she's got a hundred men. You know what she calls you? Cliff once told me. Slobs and mugs.'

'I know. Don't talk about her.'

'You have helped me. I couldn't have done without you. And I haven't really given you a damned thing, because you deserve it all . . . Simon isn't well, you know.'

I kissed her. 'Stop it. I don't want anything.'

'You only want that rotten little whore.' There is no bitterness in her voice. It's useless to be bitter about facts.

Yes, I want that rotten little whore. I don't want anyone else. And I never had any illusions about her. To be fair, she never went out of her way to conceal what she was. Or was she just a romantic, looking for what she called the perfect fuck? Whore was never the right term for her – or nymphomaniac either. She was a travelling woman who every so often would fancy settling down; and who always had to move on.

In the meantime I worked hard, took out girls from time to time, but not from Droylsden's, and got nearer and nearer to Davina and, through her, to Clifford. I was aware that Sheila was his mistress, but he behaved himself in working hours and Davina who, God knows why, always felt guilty about her accident, saw it as being purely physical. Anyway, she accepted it. What she could not accept was when it turned serious. That was the time when the Merchandising Manager fell ill.

And that is where I came in. I am not very proud of it either. Sometimes I think that what happened to me afterwards served me right. Can I manage to bring that out too? Can I look at it? There's so much I can't look at. I can look at all my business transactions without the faintest twinge of guilt. Contrary to what a lot of people suppose, the retail business is honest. A crooked buyer generally ends up in jail or jobless. And any organisation which promotes otherwise than on merit is in trouble sooner or later. I was in fact the best man for the job, I was promoted on merit. But that's not how it appeared to a lot of people.

Simon was elected to put the offer to me. For reasons of security, I suppose, we had lunch in London, at the Hostaria Romana in Dean Street; it was a cold but bright and sparkling October day, and I had seafood cocktail and liver which did actually melt in the mouth, following it up with profiteroles smothered in cream because that day I was in a mood for indulging myself. We shared a bottle of hock and I had a Strega with my coffee; I have never enjoyed a meal more. For I felt that everything was going my way, that the promotion was purely on merit. Simon had the figures at his finger-tips, and they were figures to be proud of: I had doubled the profits of the men's-wear department since I came, and they were still rising.

'You have *energy*, you have *vision*, my dear Jim,' Simon said. He patted my hand, something he was given to doing with all personable young men. 'Why, I get *my* clothes from Droylsden's now – and, believe me, I'm hard to please. I'll tell you the truth: the men's-wear department was in a rut. A deep *deep* rut, my dear. You heaved it out.' He patted my hand again; he had a plump white hand and it was very hot and moist. 'Oh, we rub along. We've been there a long time and we sell sound merchandise. But changes are needed . . .' He scrutinised his gleaming finger-nails, holding the fingers straight out instead of doubling them. 'And problems have to be sorted out. Very *delicate* problems.'

'What have you in mind exactly?'

'There's a very distinct possibility that my brother may make a fool of himself. In the classic way. Over a young woman.'

I was still enjoying the fact of my promotion and the strawberry taste of the Strega and the black bitter coffee and the taste of my cigarette – I was trying to cut down and it was the first of the day. 'You mean his secretary?'

He nodded. *'Disgusting!'* He grinned. 'Well, love, disgusting to me anyway.' The little spurt of truthfulness endeared him to me. 'However, there it is. The affair has gone on for quite a while now, and none of us took it seriously. As you know' – he wagged his finger at me – 'you do have a rather special relationship with Davina, don't you, you *cunning* boy? However, he wants to marry her.'

'Jesus! That'd be complete disaster.' I stubbed out my cigarette and lit another.

'There are wheels within wheels. Some people on the Board aren't happy about Davina being the *eminence grise.* Personally, I'm all for leaving well enough alone. The present arrangement works.'

'Have you had a word with him about it?'

'I tried to, but he's most evasive. I thought of sacking the young lady, but that might make things worse. My impression is that Cliff would be glad to have matters taken out of his hands.'

My mouth had turned dry and I suddenly wished that I'd not eaten so much. 'And how would you do that?'

'Would you care for another Strega?'

I shook my head. 'I'd like you to be more explicit, Mr Droylsden.'

164

'Simon, my dear Jim, Simon. Well, you're now Merchandising Manager at an early age. You're a personable young man. The young lady's quite pretty, very clever – a little wild perhaps, but who cares about that these days?'

'I see. Supposing she doesn't like me?'

'I've made a few inquiries. I think she does.'

'My God, you have it all cut and dried, don't you? And I thought that I'd got the job because I was the best man –'

'So you are, my dear, so you are.' He patted my hand. 'If she won't play ball, it doesn't matter. Our offer still stands.'

And so the good moment became a bad moment and I went back to my office with a violent pain in my stomach and a violent headache and at half-past four had to go home and straight to bed. I knew that I had the job whatever happened, but I also knew that if I failed to do what they wanted me to do, then, whatever they said, they'd find some way to make things turn sour on me.

And the consequence was that a fortnight later Sheila lay naked beside me in my bedroom in the flat; I tried to stop thinking as she took my penis in her hand, and then, taking me by surprise, I had my orgasm and rolled away from her. That, it seemed was the end of the road for me. How long would it be before she told someone? How long would it be before everyone at Droylsden's knew? How long before everyone in the town knew? And what, despite all the assurances of Simon to the contrary, would it do to my security of tenure there? I got out of bed and looked for my underpants.

'Where are you going?' Sheila asked.

'I'll take you home.'

'Come back to bed. Don't be so damned silly.'

I obeyed her, but kept a little apart from her, as far as I could in a three-quarter bed. I sat up in bed, the head-board cold against my naked back, shivering uncontrollably. I took a cigarette from the bedside table and lit it.

'I'm sorry. I'm no bloody good, that's all.'

She sat up besides me and took the cigarette from me. Her face was quite calm. 'You are an idiot.' She put her arm around me. 'You're shivering. Calm down.'

I lit a cigarette, my hand shaking so much that the match went out at the first attempt.

'I'm sorry. That's all I can say. I'm sorry.'

'Life's too short to be sorry. What are you worrying about? It happens to lots of men.'

It happens to lots of men; miraculously I stopped shivering.

'You won't think very much of me just the same.'

'Don't be stupid. What good would that do?' Suddenly she touched my now shrunken penis.

I moved away. 'Now you'll think I'm a bloody freak.'

'What's it matter as long as it stands up at the proper time? I think it's cute.' She grabbed me again. 'It only needs warming up. It's just like Cliff's . . .'

'Just like Cliff's?'

'Do you think you're unique?' I liked having her hand there: I had never known a greater sense of relief.

'I feel such a bloody fool,' I said.

'Don't worry. Don't hurry. We've got all night. Just relax. You're not in a competition, are you? There's nobody here but us. Just lie still. We don't have to go anywhere . . .'

And we lay still and we stroked each other, very gently, and then she put my hand between her legs and I concentrated upon giving her pleasure, forgetting myself, and then almost without realising it I was inside her, thrusting, stiff, a man at last, back to the human race and, as, gasping, I had my orgasm, aware that if I never had sex again it didn't matter, it couldn't be taken away from me: I was a man.

And that is where the love story began. I told her lies afterwards, of course. I didn't tell her that this was the first time. I didn't thank her for what she had done for me. I did say it was marvellous, but I didn't say just why it was marvellous. In the strict, moral sense this was wrong; in the interests of self-preservation it was right. I knew the morning after that she had enough power over me as it was.

We were married five months after that. We had a white wedding at the Anglican church and a honeymoon in Malta; I think that it was her sense of humour as much as anything else which made her insist upon the white wedding.

Gareth was begotten on our honeymoon. He wasn't an accident. Neither was Sharon. Sheila is nothing if not thoroughgoing: she decided to get married and to settle down, and having children was part of settling down, so there was no point in putting it off.

'Do you really love me?' she asked me when I proposed to her.

'I'm sure of it.'

'Poor sod. I don't really love you. But I like you.'

She put my hand between her legs; we were in bed at the time.

'Will you marry me then?'

'It won't always be like this when we marry. People get used to each other.'

'I want to marry you.'

'I think I ought to marry you. I think you'd make a good husband. And you're not married already, which helps . . .'

'I do love you, I really do. Do you want children?'

'Oh. Oh yes. Further up.' She was gripping my wrist so hard that it hurt. 'I'll give you children . . .' She sighed with pleasure. 'Do you remember what I told you when first we met?'

'I'm a mug, aren't I?' I was beginning to grow more and more excited, more and more happy. 'I don't care.'

'Not now you don't, darling. Not now . . . But later you'll be sorry . . .'

'Sorry for loving you?'

The white walls, the orange fitted carpet, the white three-quarter bed with the green and orange candlewick bedspread now tumbled on the floor, the Medici 'Massacre of the Innocents' and the Picasso Blue Period 'Mother and Child' – the old monster could be tender once – the white bedside cabinet with the white 'phone, the bright orange whitewood wardrobe with the doors which never would stay closed; plunging down now, giving, loving, *beyond* happiness now, *beyond* the memories, *past* being hurt, *past* hearing again my uncle's voice, my mother's voice whimpering; and saying again and again as I plunged, as I triumphed, as I knew that I had endured, I had *won*, saying it again and again, *I'll never be sorry*. And her voice sadly but calmly, a long time after: *You will be sorry, Jim, you will, you will, you'll wish that you'd never met me* –

And I forgot it for a long time because I was happy. She has so much to give, she's such a marvellous bitch with such a marvellous bitter tongue, she's always so much *alive*, she doesn't give a damn what she says, she has a quick, lively, impatient mind, she should have gone to the university, not me, but she never bellyaches about it, she never feels sorry for herself. When we were engaged and throughout bearing Gareth and Sharon she changed only in one way: there was no other man but me. Of that I am sure. Whatever social life we had, we had together; but most of our leisure was spent on our own.

I remember one evening, after Gareth had been put to bed, we were sitting together reading. That was in our first house, a three-bedroomed pebble-dash semi in a small development about a mile from the town centre.

She looked up and said suddenly: 'When I was first in love with you I was so fine and brave. For miles around the wonder grew. How well I did behave . . .'

'That's pretty,' I said.

'I won't keep it up,' she said. 'As the bishop said to the actress. You're quite the nicest mug I've ever met. But you'll be sorry one day . . .'

'I'll take the risk.'

'Pay no attention. You looked so complacent, I just thought I'd stir things up a bit . . .' She was quiet for a moment. 'I think I'd like another baby. I'm not getting any younger.'

And so there was Sharon. Sheila had an easy birth with Gareth, though he was a big baby, just over ten pounds. Sharon was premature, and gave her a lot of trouble and pain, and was just short of six pounds. When I held her in my arms at the nursing-home I was frightened. She was so light that I felt she'd blow away; and when I held her closer I felt that I'd break something.

Sheila looked at me with what seemed to be real dislike. She was very pale and there were dark circles under her eyes.

'You rotten sod!' she said. 'You can have the next one your bloody self.'

I took no notice because I was too absorbed in looking at Sharon, whom I had now put back very gently in her cot. I had never known that any human being could be so delicate and fragile. Gareth had had a lot of black hair and a bad-tempered expression; he had seemed more like a new-born animal than a human, sturdy and aggressive, fit almost to cope for himself, to fight for his share of food. But Sharon had to be looked after, to be cherished. I don't mean that I didn't love Gareth, but it was a different kind of love; he was somehow more a projection of me.

I have that, and I can still leave the whisky alone. I have a son and a daughter, so I can always love with a *giving* love. It's the one thing, besides my work, which has saved me in the past, it's the one thing which saves me now.

Yes, there is more. And now I have to drink the whisky. Whilst I am drinking it I will be aware only of its taste, smooth yet abrasive, sweet but almost rank, the difference between the cold of the ice-cubes and the heat in my stomach. And then there will be, for a brief while, an absence of emotion, nothing at all but the sun in Cliff Droylsden's office, showing up the wrinkles on his face without remorse; and the slack mouth, and the sweat on his forehead and the empty bottle of vodka on the desk. He was half asleep, his feet up on the desk, mumbling to himself.

That must have been about six months after the birth of Sharon. Sheila had taken to going out by herself one night a week. I've forgotten, or I choose to forget, what her excuse was then. I choose to forget. One week she went out to sit with a friend whose husband was away on a long business trip, and who was rather depressed. Another week

– in fact, most weeks – it was to meetings of the local Music Club. Sheila likes classical music; I don't. I didn't check up on her. I don't even now. Whatever it is that we have depends upon this. So I looked at Cliff Droylsden and felt nothing at all beyond a slight pity and a more than slight annoyance. I had a heavy schedule that afternoon and I was well aware why Simon had summoned me to the office.

'Can't we sober the bugger up now?' I asked Simon.

'My dear, do you think I haven't tried?'

'We could just bundle him into the Rolls and leave it to Simms.'

'He's so pissed that he'll fall out of the car. Or he'll make Simms take him to some dive or other, and then God only knows where he'll end up.' He wiped his brow with a white silk handkerchief which smelled strongly of eau-de-cologne. 'Honestly, I haven't seen him like this for *years* – ' He wrung his hands, then flapped them about helplessly for a moment, futile and fussy and even more limp-wristed than usual. 'Jim, I'm sorry, but you'll have to take him home.'

That was it. Simon was the Chairman. Three-quarters of an hour later Cliff, awake and maundering by now, was sitting on the edge of his bed at home, the housekeeper, a middle-aged woman in a black dress, hovering in the background, a faint smile on her face.

'I can manage now,' I told her. Clifford's maunderings were approaching coherence now and the less the servants knew the better.

'Are you sure, Mr Seathwaite? I've handled drunken men before, you know.'

'Quite sure. When will Mrs Droylsden return from the nursing-home?'

'In about an hour.'

'I'll stay till she returns. In the meantime I'd appreciate some coffee. A lot of coffee.'

She hesitated, then withdrew, not looking very happy about it. I didn't blame her; she saw a chance of building up her relationship with her employer, of strengthening her position, and I was going to take that advantage from her. I didn't blame her for trying.

I went to the door, where I saw a large white travelling bath-gown hanging up. It was a huge room with glossy cream walls and a king-size bed with a huge white fur bedspread. There was a door to the bathroom left of the bed. The carpeting was white and ankle-deep. I went up to Cliff with the bath-gown.

'I think you need to get your head down, Cliff. Can you manage to undress?'

He looked at me blearily. 'Of course I bloody well can.' He kicked off his shoes. 'Do you know Sean Balbriggan?'

'Naturally. It's my job to know all the buyers.'

'Big fellow with black hair and red face. A crude, ignorant Mick. Shall I tell you something about Micks?' He ripped off his tie, threw off his jacket, then tried to unbutton his shirt. He couldn't cope, and pulled it over his head along with his vest, buttons coming off in the process. 'Englishmen don't mind killing foreigners – in fact they like it – but they don't like killing Englishmen. Micks like killing Micks.'

'You mean he's in the IRA?'

'Not him. He's a slob. A real slob.'

I still didn't realise what he was getting at. There was a knock at the door and a maid appeared with a tray of coffee. It was a silver tray and the coffee service was silver. The cups, I was glad to see, were large white thick ones. I put the tray down on the bedside table and lit a cigarette. It was a fine sparkling May afternoon and I began to feel more cheerful. I might indeed learn something of value from Cliff before Davina returned – she had periodical heat treatment at the nursing-home – and so the afternoon wouldn't be entirely wasted.

When I had poured out the coffee for Cliff – I knew by now that he liked it black without sugar – he was sitting naked on the bed. I put down the coffee and handed him the bath-gown. His body was better covered up, in fact. He wasn't fat, and he had broad shoulders, but his skin was as if too loose-fitting. It sagged, all of him sagged – his face, his shoulders, his chest, his belly, his pelvis, his prick, all his muscles, all of it sagged. I took it in instantly, casually; I just as soon would not have seen it. And when he'd put the bath-gown on something struck me with extraordinary force: the limp penis was about six inches if not seven. Sheila had lied to me. And it had been a good lie, the best kind of lie; it had helped me at the time she spoke it, and it had helped me all these years, and now that it was exposed as a lie I wasn't in the least hurt, because it had served its purpose and I knew now that I was as much a man as any other man.

I helped Clifford on to the bed and put the fur coverlet over him. 'Coffee, Cliff?'

'I want a drink.'

'Have some coffee first.'

I gave him the coffee and he took a sip, the cup rattling in the saucer.

'Give me a cigarette, Jim.' I gave him a cigarette and lighted it for him. 'Jesus, I'm pissed!' He sipped the coffee. 'What the hell are you doing here?'

'I brought you home.'

'Home? More like a bloody museum. No children. *You* have two children and I've none.' There were tears in his

173

eyes. 'Sean Balbriggan. That ignorant Mick slob. She told me last night. *He* has four children. These fucking Micks breed like rabbits.'

'Shocking,' I said, humouring him. 'They'll soon out-number us.'

He was crying now, a man in his late fifties, the Managing Director of a large department stores, sitting up in bed drunk in a white towelling bath-gown, crying like a child. 'She told me in bed,' he said. 'She was laughing. *I've gone back to collecting slobs*, she said, *and a mug from time to time.* Jim, Jim, what's going to become of me?'

There was a long low Italian leather armchair by the bed; I slumped down on it. 'She was with Letty Rubins last night,' I said. 'Letty's husband's been away for three weeks in the USA.'

'Jim, what's going to become of me? Jim, I got pissed last night after she left. I had to get a taxi home. And I started again this bloody morning, Jim, this bloody morning. I've never done that before in my life.'

'You may well ask what's going to become of you,' I said in a hard voice. 'What's going to become of me?'

'You tell Davina,' he said. 'Davina will understand.'

'I hope you haven't told her,' I said. 'Or anyone else.'

'It's like catching something,' he said, still crying. 'You *catch* Sheila, it's like a cold you can't shake off.'

'It's like cancer,' I said. 'You can only cut it out.'

He wiped his eyes on his sleeve; I handed him a hand-kerchief and he squeezed it in his hand, still using his sleeve. 'Of all the bloody people,' he said. 'He's the sort of chap who's always telling you stories. Big beefy sod.'

'I think we should take the carpet out from underneath him,' I said.

Cliff looked shocked. 'You wouldn't have him sacked?'

'I'd have his balls sawn off with a rusty razor blade if I could, never mind just sack him.'

'We'll just sack him, Jim.' Davina had propelled herself into the room; I couldn't tell how long she'd been there. 'I'm sure that we can devise some way of making life thoroughly uncomfortable for Mr Balbriggan. Is there some coffee, Jim?'

I poured her a cup of coffee and lit a cigarette for her in my own mouth; I knew her well enough by now to be able to tell exactly when she needed tobacco.

'You're back early,' I said.

'A slight snag was encountered. I'm going again tomorrow.'

I pressed her hand; she smiled. 'Nothing to worry about, Jim, honestly.'

I turned towards the door. 'I'll go now. There's no point in me staying.'

'Are you going to resign?'

'There really isn't much else for me to do.'

'I thought we were friends.'

'We are friends. We always will be friends.'

'We can't really do without each other, you know. *He* can't' — she pointed towards Cliff, still crying — 'and certainly I can't. I think it's time that you grew up, Jim. Ronnie Struthers is near retiring age, and his deputy is too. Think about it.'

I was thinking of the lie that Sheila had told me the first time we'd gone to bed together; I was thinking too of what I'd come to feel for Davina and for Cliff, even for Simon. It was no good, I was overwhelmed, there was no quick answer; I went over to her and put my hands on her shoulders, drawing strength from her.

'I don't know what to think.'

Cliff's eyes were closing; I moved over and took the coffee cup and the cigarette from him.

'We'll go to my room,' Davina said. 'Let him sleep.'

'He was never jealous of you,' she said later. 'As much as there can be anything to be jealous about, there is between us ... I can't begrudge him anything. God knows he'll pay for it.'

I don't think that I answered her. I knelt down beside the bed and put my head between her breasts and stayed like that a long time; the sensation was of being given back something of which I'd been robbed. No one can understand who has not been robbed as I have been robbed; comfort, kindness, consolation, are words I use casually but delicately to describe it, rejecting the big word, the obvious word, the emotive word, and the even bigger, darker, more emotive word behind it.

And that evening I drove into London and sat for an hour over a pint in a pub in the King's Road, and was picked up by a twenty-year-old girl in blue jeans, and bought her dinner at an Italian restaurant, and was offered payment for the dinner in a small hotel near King's Cross to which she took me; and declined the payment. And was forced to decline the payment; the blue jeans and pink bikini pants were off the instant we were inside the hotel room; the young slim body was, my eyes told me, desirable, but my loins told me otherwise. I think that I knew before she picked me up, but I had to try. It was fair enough: whoever tries to use sex for revenge is bound to suffer. I lied to Sheila about it when I returned, but it didn't do me any good; she simply shrugged her shoulders and said, that she didn't blame me, if she'd been me, she'd have done the same. I've never tried again, though sometimes

I dream of finding a woman whom I can love. That is all; I don't ask that she loves me.

I've thought about our arrangement, our civilised arrangement once, and once is enough. Sometimes I fish up from my memory scraps of the talk that night; I ask myself if I could have done otherwise, if I couldn't somehow or other have persuaded her to change. I couldn't lose my temper with her. That was the odd thing. I was angry with her going home, but when I was with her the anger evaporated.

– *How could you, Sheila? How could you?*

That was the most I could manage. And my heart was beating so hard that I could scarcely get the words out.

– *Because I'm a rotten bitch. I told you you'd be sorry for loving me.*

You can't do anything about that. I could have killed her, of course, but then what would have happened to the children? Or to me? I'd then be in the hands of the police – and social workers and all that ghastly crew – and so would the children. Or in the hands of her mother and the Staffordshire relations, which would be better, but not much.

The people like me are the ones you never hear about. We bite the bullet, we *endure*. We make arrangements, we soldier on, we survive. Yes, there was a moment when I wanted to smash her smooth face in; yes, there was a moment when I wanted to waylay Sean Balbriggan and kill him, and kill him painfully. Yes, but only very briefly, there was a moment when I wanted to kill myself, to make my exit from the whole dirty mess, to give up trying. I saw a little book of funny drawings once called *Things*. Things are small malignant creatures with hairy legs; things, grinning all over their ugly faces, are generally too much for us. The illustration to 'Things Beyond Our Ken' showed a lot of things in running kit well ahead of a panting, sweating little man to whose head an arrow pointed marked *Our Ken*. That drawing has always stuck in my mind. Our Jim had been racing against things for all his life, and that day, though only for a moment, he wanted to stop running.

I suppose that I shall carry on until the end. Sometimes it appals me to contemplate the long weary way I've come and the long weary way I've still to go. I'm proud of myself in a way: I haven't cracked up, I haven't made any excuses for myself, I haven't asked anyone for help. When you look at Our Ken, he's rather a gallant figure. He's clueless, he's in terrible shape, his running shorts are baggy and nearly cover his knees, he never asked to be in the race, and he suspects that he hasn't the ghost of a chance. If by some miracle he wins, either the prize won't be worth having or else, if it is worth having, he'll be cheated of it. But as long as there's a breath in his body, as long as his short skinny legs can keep moving, Our Ken will be in there trying.

I tried to explain some of this to Davina. And she did understand. She didn't merely buy me off that afternoon. I'm well aware how it appeared to Simon. In return for not citing Cliff as co-respondent I was promised the job of General Manager. It must appear even worse to him now, because Cliff still sees Sheila from time to time. *Sees*: I mean that he still fucks her whenever he gets the chance. He doesn't tell me and Sheila doesn't tell me. No need; I always know. The day afterwards he's always a shade too bright and breezy; he looks younger. His clothes even look better; it's as if they and him had been given a thorough dry-cleaning.

I don't feel any hatred towards him; we're in the same boat. His is a simpler fixation than mine. He's tried to rid himself of it with other women, but it hasn't worked. I wouldn't even try that again after my experience with that little scrubber I picked up in the King's Road. But we're both hooked on the same drug, and a side-effect more or less isn't worth arguing about.

'I shall understand if you do cite Cliff,' Davina said to me that afternoon. 'It wouldn't alter what I feel for you.' Her arms tightened around me.

'It wouldn't serve any purpose. I can't do without her.'

That is the nearest I ever approached to telling anyone else how helpless I was to escape her.

'People like her sometimes come to a bad end.'

'It wouldn't help me if she did. She's still going to be the same. Nothing will ever touch her.' I had a mental picture of Sheila sitting by the fire, her needlework forgotten for a moment, that faint smile on her face, sleek, feminine, untouched, untouchable.

'It would be better for you if you'd never met her.'

'Oh no,' I said, horrified. 'Oh no, Davina, I can't ever say that.'

For the first time she took my hand and guided it to her belly. She was lying on the bed. I remember that she had a dark blue fine-wool button-through dress. I felt a rigid corset and hard protuberances through the corset; she guided my hand under her dress between her legs and I felt a warm moist softness. She took my hand away gently, kissed it, and smoothed down her dress. 'There isn't any way to say it.'

I kissed her on the lips. 'I know.'

'I wouldn't let anyone else do that. I wouldn't want anyone else to do that. Christ!' There were tears in her eyes, but tears of anger rather than of grief. 'If only things had been different, I'd have given that bitch a run for her money, old though I am . . .'

It sustained me later when I confronted Sheila. You'd think that I'd have been apprehensive before, that it would have been a traumatic experience, violent emotionally if not physically. But she hardly changed position in her chair or raised her voice.

'What it all boils down to,' she said thoughtfully, 'is that I've been respectable for far too long . . . And I felt sorry for poor old Cliff.'

'And *poor old* Mick Balbriggan? That ignorant Mick pig?'

She arched an eyebrow. 'Mick? I told you once I collected slobs. I needed him to complete a set.'

'I'm going to smash this particular specimen. His days at Droylsden's are numbered.'

She smiled broadly. 'He must pay for his pleasures. He knew damned well whom I was married to.'

'Do you want a divorce?'

She looked shocked for the first time. 'Whatever for? Of course one day I might meet a man who's neither a mug nor a slob . . .'

I must be a freak. Why wasn't I angry? Why did I leave it to her to talk about divorce? But the word struck cold. I was past caring about my job at Droylsden's, past caring about Davina; all I cared about was for her to be quite simply *there*.

'I'm a mug, of course.'

'Of course you are, dear. You're too decent to be anything else. It's what you were born for. Even Sharon, at her age, can wrap you round her little finger.'

'I ought to break your neck.' I don't quite know why

I said it – I've never hit a woman in my life and never will – but I wanted to frighten her, ruffle her absolute composure, even if only a little.

'There's nothing much I can do about it if you do decide to break my neck. Double glazing is pretty well soundproof.' She yawned, then lit a cigarette.

'For Christ's sake, doesn't anything move you?'

'Nothing very much. I just like to enjoy myself in my own quiet way. I'd rather be married than not. You're a damned good provider and you're kind to the kids, and you've got a good job. I'd hate to be married to a man who was no one.'

'Presumably if I lost my job you'd have no time for me.'

'As long as Davina's there you're not going to lose your job. That's another thing, since we're being so moral.' There was still no emotion in her voice. 'Some wives might well ask what goes on there.'

'Nothing that you would understand.'

'All I know is that after you've had one of your cosy tête-à-têtes with her you come home like the cat that's swallowed the cream . . . What the hell do you *do*? What *can* you do? I happen to know that below the waist she's like a road under repair . . .' Now she was smiling again. 'Jim, you're kinky, you really are . . .'

I had hoped she'd be jealous. That would have been a help. It wouldn't have altered anything, but it would have perhaps made me feel less of a pimp, given me some self-respect. But she was merely curious. Not even lewdly curious; coolly, technically, impersonally curious.

'Davina is my friend. What happens between us is my business.'

'Then what happens between me and any other man is my business.'

'Oh, for God's sake, don't let's argue like that!' I was

really angry with her now. 'It's so bloody childish, you're talking about tit for tat, not *us*, not *people* –'

'I quite agree,' she cut in. 'Let's be civilised, let's say what we really think. Just for a change. It's all such a stupid charade, this business of marriage, having just one man, for God's sake! For the rest of your life . . .' She looked at me appealingly. 'Don't *you* ever fancy anyone else?'

'No, not really,' I said, my voice dull. 'That's my problem. That's my chief problem.'

I was very near then telling her the truth. Would it have made any difference? Would she have declared her penitence, promised to be a good faithful wife in future? No, she wouldn't. Because she wouldn't have been guilty of such a thumping lie. She would have felt sorry for me. She would have understood me better than ever before. She would have understood me more fully than any human being has the right to understand another. She would have continued to live exactly as she lives now, but with the knowledge that she was hurting me in a special way against which I had no defence. And eventually guilt would have crept into a consciousness devoid of guilt before. She wouldn't have lived with this guilt – or this pity. She would have walked out and left it behind her.

I didn't believe at the time that even I should be able to accommodate myself to the situation. I even felt – half hoped for it – that I might stop loving her. Nothing is ever simple, no emotion is ever pure. I didn't want to leave Droylsden's either. I am not a very nice character. And certainly I'm not an honoured one except strictly in business hours. I wanted the job of General Manager and I enjoy it enormously. If anyone despises me for the way in which I got it, they haven't told me so yet, so I can live with it. And I have the children. Already Gareth is moving away from me, he wants to emulate me, he wants to be just like Daddy, but he doesn't want to come nearer to me; he's what they call a real boy, he's not demonstrative, he is as if ashamed of loving me. I can live with it, because Sharon loves me, Sharon shows it, Sharon makes a fuss of me, whatever love I give to her is returned a hundredfold. No doubt this will not last, and I must accept it when she finds out that she can't marry Daddy, that she will in fact marry someone else. I must be prepared to let her go. In the meantime I give love to her and she returns it. I have thought of leaving Sheila but never of leaving my children. I have hung on, I have stayed at my post like that poor sod of a soldier at Pompeii. It is as well to die at your post standing to attention, knowing that you're a man and not a frightened animal, making a *choice*, a *deliberate choice*, at the end, as it is to die screaming and wetting yourself, running to no avail, the burning lava catching you up. Our Ken, you see, is a ridiculous figure, but at least he's *behind* the Things, trying to catch them up. The Things are not *chasing* him, he is not fleeing from them. He's sick and tired and despairing, but he is not *frightened*. And maybe this is what I have instead of honour.

Now it's all out, and I lie on the sofa staring at the glass of whisky. I don't need it any more. Or the television or music or a book or a magazine. I have held nothing back, I have not spared myself. My brief sojourn in the world of Sheila's special friends I do not count, because that was one of the few times in my life when I was so drunk that I can't remember exactly what happened; there is only a vague recollection of a minstrels' gallery and kissing a woman and Sheila laughing at me, a man's arm around her waist. That doesn't count. I remember enough to know that there was in fact no orgy; the atmosphere wasn't right. I saw enough of her world not to be drawn in. When we have a party a few of them are invited under sufferance; they give flavour and bite to a party in small doses, like cayenne pepper or garlic. They are a danger for the future, but I've enough on my plate coping with the present.

What I have in my mind now is the sunflowers at the bottom of the garden, a pale yellow which somehow continues to be gaudy, as outrageous and somehow unnatural as their height, which must be near ten feet. These and lilies-of-the-valley are the flowers I like the best; I'm only sorry that they can't both flower at the same time, the lilies-of-the-valley, white and delicate, round the bases of the sunflowers. Seen like that, you'd get the most from each; in my *white* town, my *shining* town, there is a variety of lily-of-the-valley which blooms from July to September like the sunflower. (I shall still need my town, just as I shall still need every other form of escape: this moment of calm will not last forever.)

There is the sound of light footsteps and Sharon appears in her pink flowered Viyella nightdress, half asleep. I sit up and she runs into my arms and settles on my knees, burrowing closer to me with a little grunt of content. Her forehead is moist and the fair hair darkened with sweat. The sun has bleached it almost white this summer and her face has a dusting of freckles.

'What is it, love? Can't you sleep?'

'I'm thirsty, Daddy.' Her eyes closed.

'Stay there, then.' I put her down gently on the sofa, go into the kitchen, and half fill her Peter Rabbit mug from the jug of orange-squash which stands in the refrigerator. I return to her and sit down beside her, holding the mug to her lips; she's half asleep and I'm afraid that she'll spill it otherwise.

She drinks noisily. 'Where's Mummy?'

'Seeing a friend, dear.' I swallowed, fighting down a sudden rage. 'Yes, she's seeing a sick friend.'

'When will she be back?'

'Soon. Don't worry. I'll look after you. I'll always look after you.'

'And Gareth? And Mummy?'

'And Gareth. And Mummy. I'll look after you all.'

She kisses me. 'I love you, Daddy.'

'I love you.' There is no other human being to whom I can say that without qualification; I hug the warm soft little body for comfort. In a moment I must take her upstairs. I shan't carry her because, though I'm not drunk, I've had a lot to drink and if I slipped and she were hurt I'd never be able to live with myself again. That's another difference between loving a child and loving a woman: I worry all the time about Gareth and Sharon but I never worry about Sheila. I wouldn't want her to die before her time and I literally can't imagine life without her, but anyone who habitually takes other women's men and hands them back very much the worse for wear isn't, to say the least of it, a good life-insurance risk.

I don't think of it now. In a moment I'll take Sharon's hand and put her to bed. In the meantime I'm quietly happy sitting here with my arm around her. I do not want anything more just now but I am still in the race. After I have put Sharon to bed I shall return to the sofa and sit there quietly waiting for Sheila to return. I shall know that it's her Volkswagen by the sound of the gears clashing as she changes down to come into the drive. You'd think that someone so calm and competent would be a good driver, but she does terrible things to the gears; I've learned to accept it, but keep her away from my car.

As soon as I hear her footsteps – light, quick, almost dancing – outside, I'll go to the kitchen and put the kettle on. She always asks for strong coffee after she's been out. She sleeps well just the same. She will say something perfunctory about where she's supposed to have been, and I will say something perfunctory in return, and she will drink her coffee and I will finish off my whisky.

And I shall be quite happy. It *is* a love story that I've built up with the most unlikely materials. I suppose that there's a considerable element of the comic: I've often laughed at Our Ken myself. But I am a man and nothing can take that away from me. If I never have sex again, she's given me that. She spoke the releasing, healing words – *Never hurry, never worry* – and she told me that wonderful lie about Cliff. She cured me of what ailed me; it's turned out to have been a rough cure but I'll live through it.

I'm quietly happy, sitting here with my arm around my child. The road outside is bordered by plane trees and the lamps are old-fashioned wrought-iron gas-standards with fancy scrollwork which look nice even when they're not lit. They have electric lights in them instead of gas mantles, of course, but the light is warm yellow and brings out the green and brown of the trees. It's not far off midnight now and I must take the child to bed because very soon I shall hear the grating of misplaced gears and the brakes screeching as she goes into the garage, and her footsteps – light, quick, almost dancing – outside. I will look after her and Sharon and Gareth and I'll keep in that bloody race right to the end. A man can do no more than that. I say again – for the pleasure of using that simple word – a *man* can do no more than that.

**Also in Magnum Books and
Methuen Paperbacks**

JOHN BRAINE

Life at the Top

Joe Lampton is a success – or so it seems. He's married
to a rich man's daughter, has a well-paid job, and
now belongs to the wealthy class he used to envy. But
after ten years of affluent living he faces a crisis in his
life. Once again his restless drive towards other
women and material success begins to assert itself,
and Joe is ready to break out . . .

The Jealous God

Vincent Dungarvan is a young schoolmaster, thirty
years old but still a virgin. His mother wishes him to
become a Roman Catholic priest, and he himself half
believes he has the vocation. Then he meets Laura
– erotically attractive as well as intelligent, open and
warm. He passionately wants to marry her, but his
church stands as a barrier between them . . .

The Pious Agent

Introducing Xavier Flynn, fervent Catholic and
ruthless professional killer. The enemy is FIST, a
secret revolutionary group – their mission is sabotage
their target one of Britain's best-established industries.
Grappling with a ferment of intrigue, counter-
plotting and violent death demands the ultimate
degree of razor-sharp wits and ice-cool expertise. But
Xavier is a born survivor – with one eye fixed on
heaven and the other on the nearest desirable woman.

'Mr Braine is a highly welcome newcomer to the spy
story scene.'

Francis Goff, *Sunday Telegraph*

PEARL S. BUCK

The Good Earth

This world-famous novel tells the story of the farmer Wang Lung and his constant struggles against famine and destitution. The people it so beautifully describes are Chinese peasants whose very survival depends on the co-operation of nature. But even when Wang Lung overcomes the poverty which surrounds him, and achieves some measure of material success, he finds problems of a human kind still to be resolved.

Dragon Seed

Pearl Buck's very moving novel which captures all the courage and sacrifice of a peasant family under the impact of war.

'In *Dragon Seed* Miss Buck has painted a superb family group. Ling Tan the farmer, his wife, and his sons and daughters are set down with that affection and understanding which alone produces the living image.'

Time and Tide

KEN KESEY

Sometimes a Great Notion

His brilliant successor to *One Flew over the Cuckoo's Nest*

Hank Stamper has lived beside and fought with the Wakonda River in the State of Oregon all his life. The riverside house built by his father, old Henry, has become a fortress – both against the river, which after long years of erosion now swirls round three sides of it, and against the jealousies and rivalries of men. When Hank's college-educated half-brother Leland returns to his childhood home, in response to a cryptic summons, he is not sure whether Hank needs his help for the family logging business or simply wants to give him a further taste of the humiliation he knew there as a boy. In learning the answer to these questions he becomes involved in the Stamper clan's bitter battle with the union, the town and the forces of nature.

'The author's vitality is apparently boundless . . . His book is a brilliant performance'

The Times

'Raw American power . . . proud, stubborn, scornful, defiant'

Playboy

'As big and brawling as the country it describes'

Time

J. I. M. STEWART

The Gaudy

The first novel in his Oxford quintet.

On the occasion of an annual dinner, Duncan Pattullo revisits his Oxford college for the first time in many years. He meets again old friends and enemies of his undergraduate days, and as the evening passes he finds himself increasingly involved in a series of extraordinary developments that bring him closer to the new Oxford generation as well as his own.

'Wit, acute observation, clever plotting . . . As a gallery of characters it leaves nothing to be desired'
Financial Times

Young Pattullo

The second novel in his Oxford quintet.

Arriving for his first term at Oxford, the youthful Duncan Pattullo encounters the mixed collection of undergraduates who will become his friends. Characteristic Oxford rumpuses and calamities help bring together the tenants of his college staircase in incidents of unpredictable comedy blended with wry nostalgia. This is a story of the Oxford of earlier days, now gone for ever, but here recalled with deep affection.

'This beautiful novel of social manners . . . will be remembered a long, long time'
Scotsman

RONALD LOCKLEY

Seal Woman

Cut off by a high rampart of cliffs, the forgotten shoreline of Kilcalla Bay is filled with all the wild beauties of untouched nature. There a young stranger meets and falls in love with Shian, the seal girl, whose past is strangely interwoven with age-old legends about human ties with the inhabitants of the deep. As their relationship develops he decides he will accompany her when she swims with the seals to their refuge far out on the western horizon.

COLIN FREE

Ironbark

The turbulent story of Frank Gardiner, whose exploits rocked the Australian Colony.

After five cruel years of forced labour, Frank Gardiner returns to Ironbark a changed and dangerous man. They've almost forgotten him there – and his beautiful Kate has gone off and married another. Determined to win her back, he finds himself a new trade, as a bushranger robbing travellers on the roads. His violent career soon makes him the number-one outlaw. And then Frank plans the boldest robbery of them all . . .

Other top fiction available in Magnum Books

These and other Magnum Books are available at your bookshop or newsagent. In case of difficulty orders may be sent to:

Magnum Books,
Cash Sales Department,
P.O. Box 11,
Falmouth,
Cornwall, TR10 10QEN

Please send cheque or postal order, no currency, for purchase price quoted and allow the following for postage and packing:
UK: 19p for the first book plus 9p per copy for each additional book up to a maximum of 73p.
BFPO & Eire: 19p for the first book plus 9p per copy for the next six books.
Other Overseas Customers: 20p for the first book plus 10p per copy for each additional book.